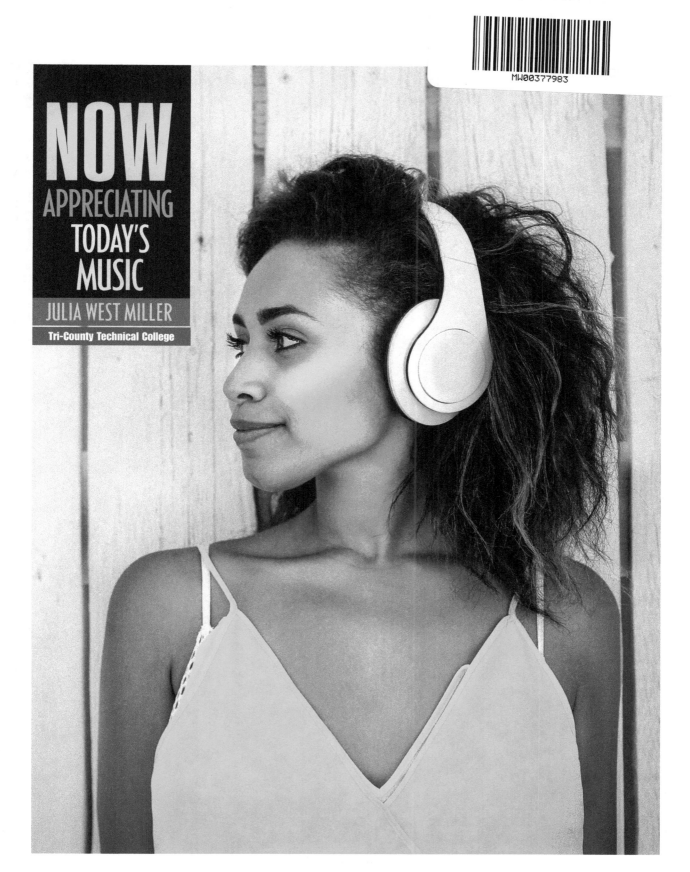

NOW
APPRECIATING
TODAY'S
MUSIC

JULIA WEST MILLER

Tri-County Technical College

Kendall Hunt
publishing company

CONTENTS

A Review of American Music from 1900 to 1950

In general, most components of American music can be traced back to the same group of roots across the Atlantic. The basics of pitch, rhythm, scales, and notation are borne of the western European traditions, as the majority of America's early settlers emigrated from a western European country. They also brought with them many folk songs, drinking songs, and folk tales that had been passed down for generations.

Another major factor in American musical tradition comes from West African rhythmic techniques brought by slaves. Though European music made use of syncopation and odd rhythms, the African techniques were much more complicated: while polyrhythms were occasionally used in European music as early as Bach, African music considered them necessary in order for music to sound complete. **Hemiola** (where a pattern of three notes is played against a pattern of two notes) was considered particularly important to African musicians, and their use of syncopation became much more detailed and complex than what could be found in the work of their European counterparts. These traditions stayed alive through the work songs and hymns sung by slaves, and eventually made their way into many American folk tunes.

America's musical traditions far predate the Revolutionary War, but military marching bands formed an important component to traditional American sound. The military is celebrated in some of America's most iconic patriotic songs (John Philip Sousa's "Stars and Stripes Forever" and "Semper Fidelis," and John Stafford Smith's "The Star Spangled Banner"). In addition, typical military marching band instruments are the most prominently featured solo instruments in jazz and blues.

Stephen Foster

One of the most important components of American music is the love of song. A number of song composers of the nineteenth century and the beginning of the twentieth century became staples of vaudeville and, when records and radio came along, staples of home entertainment as well. One of the most prominent American song composers was **Stephen Foster**, and though he died in 1864, his work was the cornerstone of American song for close to a hundred years after his death. Two of his best-known songs, "My Old Kentucky Home" and "Old Folks at Home," were chosen as the official state songs of Kentucky and Florida, respectively.

As is the case with much of American history, however, a modern view of Foster's work sheds light on the immense racism rampant in society at the time. Some of Foster's most popular songs (including "Camptown Races" and "Jeanie with the Light Brown Hair") were written for minstrel shows, in which white performers often performed in blackface. Though Foster featured black characters in his songs, they were seen through the lens of a white writer and were typically caricatures rather than fully formed characters. Though his work has been lauded as classically American, it's important to keep in mind that his songs represent an incomplete, appropriated version of black culture at the time.

Ragtime

Rather than be written about and portrayed by white artists, many black musicians proudly claimed their own voice in early American music. Much of the popular music of the early twentieth century was rooted in forms

A mural of Scott Joplin in Sedalia, Missouri, home of the Scott Joplin International Ragtime Foundation.

popularized by black performers for black audiences, but they soon caught on nationwide with all Americans. At the end of the nineteenth and beginning of the twentieth century, **Ragtime** was wildly popular. Composer Ernest Hogan was the first to have his "rags," or ragtime pieces, published in 1895. He chose to name the genre after the "Shake Rag" district in Bowling Green, Kentucky where he grew up, though the name was later attributed by some to the "ragged" syncopation in its melodies. The key characteristic that sets ragtime apart from other piano music at the time is this heavy syncopation: while the left hand of the pianist typically plays a duple-meter march-like accompaniment, the right hand plays this highly syncopated (or ragged) melody. The duality of the music, at the same time strict and playful, made it ideal for dance halls and saloons: those who wanted to dance could easily hear the beat of the music in the left hand, and those who simply wanted to listen were delighted by the playful melody in the right hand.

Though Hogan was initially credited with creating ragtime, it wasn't until **Scott Joplin** added his work to the art form that it truly took off. Joplin discovered ragtime as a traveling musician in the South. At the World's Fair in Chicago in 1893, he played numerous ragtime pieces for visitors from all over the country and the world. For many, it was the first time they'd heard music like it: it was irreverent, danceable, and infectious. Musicians visiting from out of town brought the style back to their respective cities and by 1897, it was considered the definitive form of American popular music. Several of Joplin's pieces, including "Maple Leaf Rag" and "The Entertainer," are still quickly recognized by modern Americans due to their association with American culture at the turn of the century and their use in films set in that time period. Some European composers at the time, like Erik Satie, were fascinated with the style and quoted ragtime pieces in their work when trying to evoke a typical "American" style.

Blues

Still, though Americans loved to dance to ragtime, their love of song found a home in blues music. In 1903, composer and arranger **W. C. Handy** heard a man playing a peculiar refrain on his guitar and singing repetitive lyrics. He was fascinated: some notes were flatted to give a sense of despair, the same melody was repeated every twelve measures, and the same lyrical pattern was used for each verse. The style was known as **delta blues** due to its popularity in the Mississippi delta area. Until Handy discovered it, the form was relatively unknown outside of the African American communities of the Southern United States. Handy wrote the music down and published it for the first time. This, along with migration of African Americans out of the South, led to blues becoming a nationwide phenomenon.

© Everett Historical/Shutterstock.com

Bessie Smith, a legendary Blues singer and one of the most popular early recording artists.

Blues is a unique combination of powerful vocals and a flexible group of instruments for accompaniment. The storytelling nature of the blues means, however, that less is more: the focus should be on the vocal line, with instrumentation that serves the story. A sparse guitar part can carry enough power to accompany the vocals, though brass, piano, and percussion can be included for extra emphasis. Blues songs typically follow a format now referred to as **twelve-bar blues**, referring to the typical twelve-measure length of each verse.

The vocal part in twelve-bar blues typically consists of three lines: the first line presents a problem or situation, the second line is a repeat of the first, and the final line of the verse provides a continuation of the first line or some sort of new idea to lead into the next verse. These form a statement/restatement/counterstatement style in each verse.

Blues also introduced what are typically referred to as **blue notes** to modern American music. Blue notes are notes on which the pitch is raised or lowered slightly—usually lowered, and usually by a quarter- to half-step—in order to give a sense of the singer's worry. (They're often called "worry notes" for the same reason.) It's hard to tell where this technique came from. The practice of "bending" pitches up or down exists in many folk music traditions around the world (namely English and Irish folk tunes), but its use in blues is likely derived from the work songs of slaves, where pitch and vocal intensity helped communicate feelings in coded language. Blues also introduced "swung" notes into modern American music as well. "Swinging" notes gives them an uneven feel, and specifically the practice is heard in groups of eighth notes. A pair of "swung" eighth notes would be written as such on paper, but they would be played with the rhythmic sound of a dotted eighth note followed by a sixteenth. Blues singers and players probably borrowed this practice from the heavy use of syncopation in ragtime, as a way to sound more expressive and less rehearsed.

At first, though blues was popular throughout the country, it was only popular among black audiences who attended live performances or played it themselves. W. C. Handy's blues sheet music helped spread the sound to others who might not get a chance to see it live. In 1920, Mamie Smith recorded a few of the first blues records, including "Crazy Blues," which went on to sell a million copies. Record companies took notice and got on board, making national stars out of Bessie Smith, "Ma" Rainey, and Lucille Bogan. Blues became the national sound, but its improvisational nature meant that it was constantly changing and evolving.

Jazz

The next evolution of American music was born out of elements of both blues and ragtime. **Jazz** is often referred to as "America's classical music," as it is the first broad, worldwide musical style that draws from uniquely American influences. Jazz uses ragtime's rhythmic duality: the same way a ragtime pianist would play a steady rhythm in their left hand and a heavily syncopated melody in their right hand, a jazz band has a "rhythm section" that keeps a steady beat and various solo players who provide a syncopated (often improvised) melody over the top. Jazz also borrows the blue notes and swing rhythms from blues music for further musical expression. As previously mentioned, jazz also relies heavily on improvisation: jazz soloists are typically highly skilled at their given instrument and learn how to compose melodies as they play and hear chord changes in the accompaniment.

One of the earliest popular forms of jazz is **Dixieland jazz**, or New Orleans style jazz. New Orleans was a popular port city that drew many tourists and visiting businessmen, and illicit business thrived. From 1920 to 1933, Prohibition made alcohol consumption and sales illegal. Many big cities harbored secret illegal bars known as "speakeasies." Speakeasies and brothels thrived in the seedier districts of New Orleans, and they often featured blues music to encourage patrons to stay longer, dance with each other, and ultimately rack up a larger bar tab over a longer period of time. Blues in its purest format isn't very conducive to dance, so the rhythmic elements of ragtime were added to keep things lively and fun. The rhythm section kept a steady beat, and soloists took turns improvising solos to entertain those who were taking a break from dancing or just listening. Often multiple soloists might improvise at the same time.

Soon the style extended beyond seedier venues and found its place in legal dance clubs and recording studios. The New Orleans style became immensely popular nationwide. Specifically, New Orleans style featured the previously mentioned simultaneous improvisation and the interplay between a set rhythm section and a group of soloists known as the "front line." Typically, the front line featured brass instruments like the trumpet, trombone, and tuba (or sousaphone); woodwind instruments like the clarinet and saxophone; and sometimes even string instruments like the violin. The rhythm section was often some combination of drums, guitar,

Jazz musicians perform during a Mardi Gras parade in New Orleans. Though it was one of the birthplaces of jazz, New Orleans still remains today a hotbed for jazz talent and innovation.

banjo, and double bass. Pieces in the Dixieland style were often highly syncopated and improvised versions of church hymns, gospel pieces, marches, and blues songs. Some Dixieland pieces featured vocal lines, either set to lyrics or "scat" syllables, nonsense syllables that enabled the singer to improvise creatively without having to use real lyrics.

By the time the 1930s came around, jazz was immensely profitable and was evolving yet again. Dixieland records still sold well, but jazz's acceptance among both black and young white audiences made for more profitable live concerts as well. A new form of jazz, known as **swing**, developed in this era. Swing did exactly what its name says—it utilized the swung rhythmic feel of blues instead of the more rigid ragtime tempo that inspired Dixieland jazz. Swing bands were much larger than Dixieland bands: instead of one soloist per instrument, swing bands featured several. (Swing music is also referred to as **big band** music for this reason.) Since there were multiple players per instrument, there was less room for improvisation. Listeners didn't seem to mind this: the big band sound with a swung rhythm on a catchy melody was perfect for dancing. Swing records sold well to young people of all backgrounds, and swing band concerts cleared out a space in front of the performers for dancers to show off and enjoy the music while moving their feet.

Jazz evolved in the 1940s to more prominently feature singers, specifically those with a smooth, mellow sound known as **crooners**. Crooners like Frank Sinatra, Nat King Cole, and Bing Crosby were radio staples: their music was still danceable and lively like swing, but with more of an emphasis on the vocal line. Previous big band stars like Glenn Miller evolved with the trend, featuring singers with the band. It was by this time that audiences were losing interest in instrumental music and sought compelling stories in addition to a good rhythm and melody. Instrumental jazz faded from radio play and popular favor by the beginning of the 1950s.

Swing dancing was a national phenomenon in the 1930s and 1940s at concerts with a live band and at parties with records.

The 1950s and Early 1960s: Rock, "Race Records," and the Civil Rights Movement

For years, American art, especially music, was separated down the racial lines of "white" and "black." After the emancipation of slaves, many Americans still harbored deep racial prejudices. In order to continue to exert power over minorities, white Americans passed laws to segregate public services for white Americans and Americans of color. Usually, the services provided for people of color were of much lower quality: white students were given newer textbooks and resources while students of color were given those that were out of date and falling apart; white school buildings were newer and kept in good repair while students of color attended school in older and run-down buildings; white citizens sat at the front of city busses and citizens of color were made to sit in the back. Though these services were, in fact, separate, they were by no means equal.

Many in the black community, and their white allies, were fed up. In addition to political action, they produced art and music that not only enlightened people to these problems but inspired them to act. Using music as a means to change has been present in African American history since slaves sang work songs and lullabies with coded messages about escaping to freedom. Several of these original slave song melodies made their way into later gospel songs, blues songs, and protest songs sung at civil rights marches and rallies. For instance, the song known as "We Shall Overcome" served as a rallying cry for peaceful protest:

We shall overcome, we shall overcome
We shall overcome, some day
Oh, deep in my heart, I do believe
We shall overcome some day.

Source: Charles Albert Tindley "We Shall Overcome" 1900.

The melody, lyrics, and title of this song have changed many times since its original printing, but the melody most widely known today is actually adapted from the opening refrain of a slave song titled "No More Auction Block for Me":

No more auction block for me
No more, no more
No more auction block for me
Many thousands gone

Source: Gustavus D. Pike "No More Auction Block for Me" 1873.

The use of a melody known to evoke images of slavery and past oppression is not a coincidence. Music was a useful tool to remind those fighting for racial equality just how far they'd come, and how far they had to go.

Gospel

Gospel music was heavily represented in the music of the 1960s civil rights movement. Gospel is vocal music with Christian lyrics, dramatic, loud vocals and strong rhythmic drive. Gospel flourished in the early twentieth century and into the mid-twentieth century within the Pentecostal church. These churches encouraged their members to bring in whatever instruments they had on hand, and usually this meant the instruments of the typical jazz or blues rhythm section. This led to a form that sounded like popular music, but with a sacred message.

© Melanie Lemahieu/Shutterstock.com

Gospel often makes use of multiple powerful voices at once, usually with the call-and-response technique popular in blues and jazz.

Gospel vocals are derivative of the blues style, with a raw, soulful, rough edge to them in order to portray as much emotion as possible alongside the moving lyrics. Lyrics in gospel songs are based on, or sometimes exact copies of, earlier church hymns. Some gospel melodies are even adapted from the work songs of slaves, which frequently made religious references. Gospel vocalists often employ the **call-and-response** technique popular in jazz and blues: one voice would sing the lead part, and others would respond in harmony.

Gospel has gone through many changes since its first boom in popularity in the early twentieth century. At first, gospel was an exclusively sacred form reserved for audiences in predominantly black churches, but its style and influence can be felt in the soul records of the 1960s, the vocals of 1970s disco, 1990s rhythm and blues, and even today in modern pop.

Mahalia Jackson

Mahalia Jackson, considered the most iconic gospel singer of all time, is also regarded one of the most important figures in the civil rights movement. Jackson was born Mahala Jackson in New Orleans in 1911, but she added an "i" to her first name when she started to sing professionally. She was deeply religious and sang in her church choir for years, but she also found herself drawn to popular blues artists, like Bessie Smith. Though she originally wanted to be a nurse, she loved music and believed in its ability to change hearts and minds. Eventually she met Thomas A. Dorsey, a gospel composer. Dorsey would write songs for Jackson and the two began touring together, putting on gospel concerts for largely black audiences. She developed a devoted black following throughout the 1930s, but she didn't truly break through to national stardom until the 1947 release of her song "Move On Up a Little Higher." From then on, she was known to both black and white audiences—and she eventually put on a concert for a fully integrated audience at Carnegie Hall in 1950, performed on The Ed Sullivan Show in 1956, and she even sang for the inauguration of President John F. Kennedy in 1961.

© Everett Historical/Shutterstock.com

Dr. Martin Luther King Jr.'s 1963 March on Washington, where Mahalia Jackson sang.

Jackson strongly felt that gospel music had the power to move people and to change their world views. With her new, larger audience, she eventually became heavily involved with the work of Dr. Martin Luther King, Jr. She used her fame to bring cross-cultural awareness to his message of peaceful protest.

Mahalia Jackson's career would continue to be intersectional and international, but perhaps one of her most important performances was in 1968 at Dr. King's funeral, singing his favorite hymn, "Take My Hand, Precious Lord." Adding her voice to his movement helped to build a tradition for later artists whose political beliefs were a strong driving force in their careers.

Early Rock Records

The roots of what would later become rock and roll can be seen as early as the danceable beats of ragtime, but its most powerful influence was the **rhythm and blues** music of the 1940s. Rhythm and blues was built largely on the frame of blues music's statement-restatement-counterstatement verses and the instrumentation of jazz, but with a louder, more prominent rhythm section and stronger vocals that resembled gospel. Bringing out the rhythm made the music easier to dance to, and as audiences were getting tired of dancing to swing, rhythm and blues swept in and replaced it with a cool, hard edge.

Rhythm and blues hasn't always been easy to identify. *Billboard* originally used it as a term to refer to any music marketed to black consumers, replacing the earlier term "race records." Anything by a black performer, and intended for black audiences, was usually sold in record shops in predominantly black neighborhoods as it wasn't expected to appeal to white music fans. This wouldn't last long, however. Teenagers in the 1950s, who were purchasing an average of two records a month, caught wind of the new sound and made their way to record shops in droves. Soon, rhythm and blues was popular among all young people, regardless of their racial background.

Covers

Many older white Americans still held strong racial biases and disapproved of their children listening to music that they found inappropriate. Record companies could feel the backlash and, not wanting to hurt their profits, they found what they thought was an appropriate solution: covering. **Covering** is the practice of having another artist perform a slightly different version of an original song. Covering still takes place today, usually as a tribute to the original piece or performer, but in the 1950s and 1960s it was done as a way to cater to white audiences. Songs originally written or performed by a black artist were often quickly covered by a white performer in a simpler, more clean-cut style that appealed more to white parents. Often this would result in the original performer getting no recognition from their own work, and the white cover artist selling millions of copies of a song they didn't write.

Famous Covers

One of the most notorious examples of a covered song is "Hound Dog" written by Jerry Leiber and Mike Stoller. The song was originally written for rhythm and blues singer Willie Mae "Big Mama" Thornton. Thornton's original version was released in 1953 and topped the Billboard Rhythm and Blues charts for seven weeks. Thornton's version of the song is told from the perspective of a woman throwing out her selfish, lazy boyfriend and makes several covert sexual innuendos. As the song proved popular, many unauthorized covers and copies began to circulate. Many groups took the basic melody of the song and wrote slightly different lyrics; some even wrote responses from the "Hound Dog's" perspective.

The record sold quite well in black neighborhoods, but Leiber and Stoller knew they were missing out on sales opportunities with white audiences. Since they owned the rights to the song, they sold it to several other groups before it finally became a hit for Elvis Presley in 1956. Elvis's version did what most covers at the time did: the instrumentation was pared down with acoustic instruments, the vocal was less dramatic, and the lyrics were changed to reflect teenage love rather than an adult relationship. Ultimately, although Elvis insisted that his version was a dedication to Thornton, Elvis's version sold millions of copies and catapulted him to national fame, while Thornton has said she only made $500 from her version's sales.

Covers weren't always a bad thing for the original artist. In 1955 Fats Domino, a black rock and roll singer, released "Ain't That a Shame," which reached the top 10 in the mainstream Billboard charts. Pat Boone, a white artist, released a cover of the song later that year hoping to sell his record to white audiences. Though the song

Though parents weren't originally on board with his suggestive dancing, Elvis's overall clean-cut image was ultimately quite marketable.

was a hit for Boone, it actually had the effect of driving more listeners to purchase Fats Domino's original version. Eventually, the original became far more popular than Boone's cover, and Domino earned large royalties from the sale of Boone's record as he was the original copyright owner.

Rock and Roll for Teens

Regardless of who was performing, teenagers were drawn to rock and roll. While their parents danced to swing, teens in the 1950s and 1960s wanted their music to push boundaries and make statements. Rock and roll spoke to their need to stand out and challenge authority. Songs like "Yakety Yak" by The Coasters pick up on this: told from the perspective of a teenager listening to his father list off the chores he has to do, the main character responds by mocking his tone and largely ignoring him. In "Crazy Man, Crazy," Bill Haley sings of the need to let loose and "find . . . a band with a solid beat" to which he can dance. Writing a song for young, rebellious teenagers was a reliable way to make a solid hit, and the most popular bands at the time relied upon this demographic for solid commercial success.

Soul and Motown

Despite rock and roll's appropriation of rhythm and blues for a younger generation, older black audiences who were loyal to rhythm and blues from the start still longed for that original sound. **Soul**, a form of rock and roll with a gospel-inspired vocal and hints of jazz instrumentation, fed the need for an alternative to youth-focused rock and roll as the 1960s rolled around. Prominent soul artists like James Brown and Aretha Franklin continued where rhythm

The original house where Berry Gordy, Jr. started Motown Records in Detroit, Michigan.

and blues left off. Strong voices, danceable beats, and brass solos all blended to create music that catered to black audiences that had seen their favorite artists of the 1950s get covered by white rock and roll bands and largely forgotten.

Heading into the 1960s, music was far less segregated, but the lines were still there. Black performers were still breaking into the mainstream, but covers were still commonplace. It was far more likely that a black artist's records would only be sold in mostly black neighborhoods, unless they had proven to be strong sellers in all markets. This division seemed insurmountable to many in the music industry, but to Berry Gordy, Jr., it looked like an opportunity. In 1959, Gordy founded Motown Records in Detroit, Michigan. Motown was largely focused on signing black artists singing soul music, but Gordy hired songwriters and composers who could give this soul a more universal appeal. Often this meant toning down the pitch range and roughness of the vocal line and writing softer, more lush instrumental parts. Berry also went to great lengths to control the artists' public images so that they came across as clean-cut and palatable to older audiences and white parents. Essentially, Gordy did what white artists had been doing in their covers of black artists' work for years. This softer, more commercial form of soul was infectious; Motown signed and discovered some of the most influential artists of the twentieth century, including Marvin Gaye, Diana Ross and the Supremes, Stevie Wonder, and The Jackson 5. Many of these Motown artists used their initial fame to launch into new genres later in their careers: Stevie Wonder became an important figure in the funk of the 1970s and Michael Jackson, the lead singer of the Jackson 5, became the leading figure in pop music for nearly four decades.

By the start of the 1960s, rock and roll had become the default sound of American youth. Though it had already grown to accommodate a wide variety of styles, rock grew into an even broader umbrella of subgenres that reflected a decade of political and social change.

After the first wave of rock and roll subsided in the mid-1960s, a new crop of young people added their thoughts and tastes to the national musical melting pot. This group came of age with civil rights marches, the assassinations of President John F. Kennedy and Dr. Martin Luther King, Jr., and the threat of nuclear war, so they had new ideas about peace, equality, and revolution. As the United States became increasingly involved in the Vietnam War in the late 1960s, many young Americans vocally opposed it. As civil rights proponents did in the previous decade, these young people used art and music to express their political beliefs and motivate people to change. Many became a part of the "hippie" subculture. **Hippies** were dedicated to living free, open lives and fighting for peace and justice. They embraced Eastern spirituality, anti-war sentiments, wild artistic experimentation, and recreational drug use as a means to self-discovery. Hippies dug into the roots of American folk music, blended it with rock, and created a new style to express their desires for a free, peaceful world.

Folk Revival

In the late nineteenth and early twentieth centuries, folk songwriters like Woody Guthrie and Joe Hill wrote some of the most popular American folk songs of all time. Their lyrics were deep and poetic, and they sought to expose the difficulties of the working class. Many of these songs became rallying cries for the American labor movement, demanding better conditions, higher wages, and safer workplaces.

This same spirit found a new home in the **folk rock** of the 1960s and early 1970s. Having seen music as a powerful force for change in the labor movement and the civil rights movement, those who sought to raise awareness about the Vietnam War and bring about peace saw music as a way to engage people like they never had before. Folk rock artists left behind the heavy electric guitar and drum sound of early rock and instead opted for the softer sound of acoustic guitar and light percussion. The raw, gospel-inspired vocal style of early rock was still popular in some forms, but folk vocals were lighter, more reminiscent of country and western. Lyrics were no longer aimed at restless teenagers who wanted to dance—those teenagers had grown up and were now politically and socially aware. Artists who shared this awareness were some of the most influential of the time period, like Bob Dylan.

Bob Dylan

Bob Dylan was born in 1941 in Duluth, Minnesota. He grew up on the early wave of rock and roll—he even impersonated Little Richard on the piano at school—and eventually he started his own rock bands. He cycled through a few pseudonyms and a few different styles until he discovered folk legend Woody Guthrie's music. In his first year at college, he began playing folk- and country-tinged rock songs, and by the end of that year he had made the decision to drop out. He moved to New York in 1960 and finally met Guthrie, who was in the hospital there. Dylan visited Guthrie in the hospital on a regular basis and the two formed a deep connection. It seems this spurred Dylan on to write and perform as frequently as possible, and the next year he was signed to Columbia Records.

Bob Dylan's career has continually shaped music for decades, but his blend of folk and rock in the 1960s was particularly influential.

Dylan's first album on Columbia was mostly covers, but it cut an impressive figure: his nasal, yet gravelly voice sounded almost spoken and captured the passion and spirit of the working man. For the first half of the decade, his unique blend of folk set down roots for the much of the music of the hippie movement. In the middle of the decade, even though others had begun to emulate his style, Dylan felt the need to explore more musically. Though he later incorporated more electric guitar and heavier instrumentation into his music, it was his folk style that had the biggest influence on this time period in music.

Folk Rock as a Social Statement

Inspired by Dylan, many artists sought to create their own folk-tinged styles of rock with political meaning in the same style. One of the earliest songs of the anti-war movement was P.F. Sloan's "Eve of Destruction," most famously performed by Barry McGuire. Released in 1965, the song was recorded in one rough take but took off to startling success. Sloan and McGuire capitalized on the burgeoning folk rock sound that Dylan had popularized earlier and used it as a backdrop for the dramatic, emotional plea for peace. McGuire's voice sounds much like Bob Dylan's with a raspy, gruff edge to echo the raw honesty of the lyrics. The instrumentation is derivative of the folk trend as well, prominently featuring an acoustic guitar during the verses and a harmonica, another favorite of Dylan, during the bridge. Due to its graphic lyrics, many radio stations had issues playing the song and many banned it and pro-war groups promoted boycotts of it.

However, this negative attention actually brought more awareness to the song and caused it to sell even faster. Young people saw that while it angered older, more conservative listeners, it also caused people to talk and think about the war. To show their support, anti-war protestors bought the record and called their local radio stations to request the song be played. Despite the large operation to cover the song up and discredit the artists, the song reached number one on the Billboard Hot 100 charts for the week of September 25, 1965. The movement behind the song proved that controversy, especially of a political and social nature, was actually good for business.

The Hippie Movement

P.F. Sloan and Barry McGuire's attitudes about the war, and violence in general, were shared by many in their age group. The basic ideas of the hippie movement had been around for years. The Beat Generation (later nicknamed **Beatniks**) was a group of authors in the late 1950s who used psychoactive drugs liberally and advocated for more relaxed social standards. At the turn of the 1960s, many of those who originally identified as beatniks began to become more politically involved and started referring to themselves as hippies. Hippies embraced the beatniks' drug use, especially when it came to marijuana and LSD, and also their desire for a more open, tolerant society. Hippies were much more politically and socially aware than beatniks, routinely organizing protests and rallies for political and social causes. They also changed their aesthetic: beatniks tended to dress in dark colors and don understated and simple clothing, while hippies embraced bright colors and celebrated individuality. Beatniks were largely located in Greenwich Village, a neighborhood in New York City, but the hippie movement took root in California, namely San Francisco. The transition from beatnik to hippie was evident in the music of the respective movements as well. Beatniks were drawn to the intellectual jazz sound of bebop, while hippies were drawn to a number of more expressive styles, namely folk rock and psychedelic rock.

Psychedelic Rock

Many early hippies experimented with psychedelic drugs, often in group settings or as a part of a larger artistic event or gathering. **Psychedelic rock** grew out of this communal psychoactive drug use. Psychedelic rock sought to experiment with different sounds and styles: some featured nonstandard or non-Western instruments (Indian classical instruments like the sitar often made an appearance) and extended instrumental breaks or "jams" were also popular. Some psychedelic rock was lighter with influences from the beatniks' bebop, but some featured heavily distorted guitar sounds and rougher, more powerful vocals. Performances of psychedelic rock were geared to appeal to audiences who were feeling the effects of LSD or marijuana: usually a visual component, such as a light show or dance element would be included, and the music grew increasingly experimental.

Music festivals were a large component of the psychedelic rock scene. A **music festival** is a large concert that features multiple artists and usually takes place over the course of a few days. The Trips Festival, held at San Francisco's Longshoremen's Hall in January 1966, was one of the first important music festivals of the hippie movement. Featuring a number of psychedelic rock bands including the Grateful Dead and Big Brother and the Holding Company (who would acquire Janis Joplin as a lead singer later that year), the festival took place over the course of three days to sold-out crowds of 10,000. On the second night of the festival, a bag of LSD circulated the crowd. The audience, who had been asked to dress in "ecstatic" costumes, took in the sounds of the bands and the sights of a corresponding light show.

Summer of Love

Though hippie culture was beginning to take root with the Trips Festival, it didn't go national until 1967. That summer is often referred to as the **Summer of Love** in reference to the peak of the hippie movement. San Francisco's Haight-Ashbury district, considered the epicenter of hippie culture, saw its population grow from 15,000 to a peak of 100,000 in June of that year.

Many more young people were living the hippie lifestyle of psychedelic drugs, pacifism, and communal living, and those in positions of power in the music industry took notice. John Phillips, a founding member of the influential folk rock band The Mamas and the Papas, planned the Monterey Pop Festival for that summer to capitalize

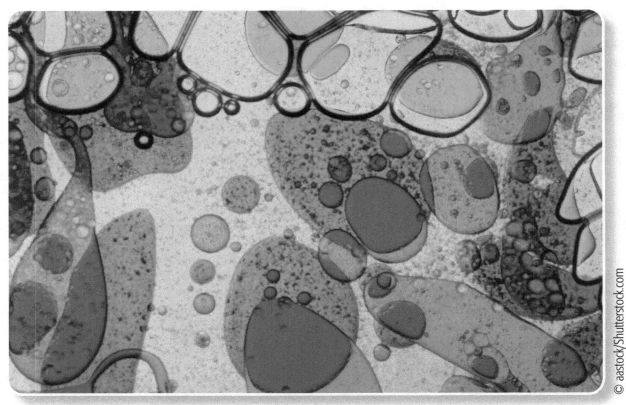

Oil projections, like this one, were popular displays at psychedelic rock concerts. Those under the influence of psychedelic drugs found them particularly appealing.

San Francisco's Haight-Ashbury district, where hippies flocked in the Summer of Love, still honors that tradition in its colorful storefronts and bohemian atmosphere today.

on the new nationwide interest. In May, Phillips wrote the song "San Francisco (Be Sure to Wear Flowers in Your Hair)" for the purpose of promoting the festival the next month. Though the song sounds like a simple folk rock hippie anthem, it was carefully crafted to attract young people to the festival and to encourage them to behave lawfully there. (The song's title also spawned the nickname "flower child" to refer to hippies.) The Monterey Pop Festival was planned quickly but quite well. The crowd of concertgoers reached 8,500 at its official peak, but as many as 90,000 were reported to have gathered around the sides of the fairgrounds where they were held. The relaxed lyrics of "San Francisco" seemed to have a real effect on the crowd: very few incidents required police intervention and some police officers even allowed the revelers to decorate them with flowers as well.

Jimi Hendrix

The Monterey Pop Festival was the first time a large American audience was introduced to Jimi Hendrix. Hendrix was already popular among British audiences, scoring three top-ten hits in the UK the previous year, but he hadn't broken through to audiences in his home country just yet. James Marshall "Jimi" Hendrix was originally from Seattle, Washington, but he moved to Tennessee in his early twenties. He began his career there playing backup for the Isley Brothers and later, Little Richard. While working for other musicians, he also took time to develop his own style. Hendrix grew up on the music of blues legends Muddy Waters and B.B. King. He fused this blues sound with the rock and roll that was popular at the time, eventually pushing them both to the extreme.

© Max Herman/Shutterstock.com

A bronze statue to Jimi Hendrix's legacy in his hometown of Seattle, Washington.

His performance at the Monterey Pop Festival put him on the map as a rebellious, hard rocker with outrageous style and even more outrageous stage antics. Hendrix's musical style was new to the American music scene: not only was he a virtuoso on the guitar, but he applied a number of electronic effects like vibrato, a wah-wah pedal, and gritty distortion that would later become staples of the punk and heavy metal scenes of the 1970s. Hendrix finished his set in Monterey by dousing his guitar in lighter fluid, lighting it on fire, smashing into the stage, and throwing it into the audience. It was a performance that wouldn't soon be forgotten, and Hendrix and his band The Jimi Hendrix Experience became overnight sensations in the United States. Sadly, Hendrix's death from drug-related causes three years later would coincide with what many considered the end of the hippie movement.

By the beginning of 1968, hippie culture was largely appropriated by the mainstream and had lost its rebellious edge. Though the style was losing steam, the image and sound were still profitable for bands and record companies. Music festivals were still quite lucrative as well, and as a result many more were planned in the last few years of the 1960s.

Woodstock

In the summer of 1969, a group of four businessmen conceived of the Woodstock Music and Art Fair. Often referred to simply as "Woodstock," it was originally planned as a three-day, paid concert on a dairy farm in rural New York. The planning process was severely hindered by changing locations and planning issues. Three days before the show was supposed to begin, the organizers realized their resources were too limited to complete the entire project. The choice had to be made between finishing the building of the stage or building fences and ticket booths to keep unpaid audience members out. Attendees began coming in the tens of thousands the next day, and because there were no fences built yet, coordinators were forced to provide free entry to all who showed up. The large influx of concertgoers effectively shut down the small town and caused a number of traffic jams, and the governor even threatened to call in National Guard troops to help keep the young revelers in line. Though the planning was frantic and the resources were far too low for all of the attendees, the festival itself actually went quite well and very little police intervention was needed.

Among the groups and artists who performed at the festival were the Grateful Dead, Santana, Janis Joplin, The Who, Joan Baez, Jefferson Airplane, Jimi Hendrix, and Arlo Guthrie.

Altamont

The Altamont Speedway Free Festival, held at the Altamont Speedway in California, drew a sharp contrast to the free and fun atmospheres of the Monterey and Woodstock music festivals. Grace Slick, the lead singer of Jefferson Airplane, said that when her band arrived to perform, "I had expected the loving vibes of Woodstock but that wasn't coming at me. This was a whole different thing." Slick's intuition would prove correct. The audience was rather calm during the first set by the band Santana. Later, though, the scene devolved into scattered drug-fueled violence. A number of fights broke out, cars were stolen, members of numerous bands were assaulted, and one audience member was stabbed to death in front of the stage during the Rolling Stones' set.

The hippie era of the Monterey Pop Festival, with its gentle people and flowers, was officially over after Altamont. Music festivals became increasingly rare for years afterward, and the hippie trend slowly filtered out of popular culture. Many young hippies now looked to find stable jobs and had to abandon the ideals they held dear in the Summer of Love.

Though the hippie movement had largely died out at the end of the 1960s, its culture of inclusivity and equality left quite a mark on the music industry. Going into the 1970s, the hard racial lines of previous music eras had largely faded away, leaving new genres that borrowed freely from a wide variety of musical traditions.

At the turn of the 1970s, hippies had largely fallen out of fashion though the ideals that they championed were still alive and well. Young Americans still felt a need to protest against war and find new outlets of expression. More still continued to push for a more open, permissive society that welcomed racial integration and accepted people of all sexual orientations. Even the trend of freestyle dancing in large groups to live or recorded music, originally made popular by hippies at music festivals, was still wildly popular. Though the hippies had moved on, their ideals thrived in the decade's new counterculture movements, and many of them gave life to what would later become known as **disco**.

Disco's Roots

In the late 1960s and early 1970s, Philadelphia's Latino and black communities had adopted the hippies' trend of freely dancing in large groups during concerts or to prerecorded music. The trend was adopted as a backlash to the perceived "white-washing" of rock: most lead singers of popular rock bands were white men and geared their music toward the same. Coupled with the rise of Motown as an alternative to the white-appropriated rock, members of the black and Latino communities in major cities started to move toward a smoother, more dance-oriented sound that felt open and welcoming. Bands like Sly and the Family Stone, and previous Motown acts like Diana Ross and the Supremes, eagerly produced new music that drew a huge contrast to the hard edges of psychedelic rock. Their music featured smoother male vocals, or powerful female gospel-style vocals, as opposed to the hard-edged male vocals most often included on rock tracks.

The addition of orchestral instruments, such as a flute melody or even sections of strings as accompaniment, drew further contrast. The sounds of synthesizers and electronic effects further helped to separate disco from rock and rhythm and blues.

At the same time, America's gay communities, especially those in large cities, were seeking a place to gather without prejudice. Several private clubs sprang up to host parties for gay and lesbian revelers, and bars found that catering specifically to gay patrons could be lucrative (though legally risky, as it was still illegal for two men to dance together into the late 1960s). Loud music, a dark and open dance floor, and a welcoming attitude were essential for these clubs, and the most appealing music to their patrons was disco.

The name "disco" is derivative of the French word "discotheque," referring to a dance club that played prerecorded music. (In this way, the word can be used to describe a dance club and the music played in said clubs.) The skill of blending one song into the next led to a new breed of musician: the **disc jockey**, or **DJ**. The term "disc jockey" had already been applied to radio hosts, but this breed of DJ saw their audience in person and could gauge their energy in real time. Seasoned DJs could read a crowd's reaction to a particular song and carefully pick the next to maintain the right energy in the room.

Singer Thelma Houston had sung gospel for years before a slew of disco hits in the 1970s.

While the music was an important component of a disco club, club organizers also fixated on enhancing the experience as much as possible with visuals and lighting. A typical disco featured a large sound system, a colorful (and sometimes lighted) dance floor, some form of lighting system capable of a number of dazzling effects, and a mirrored ball to scatter light around the room (also known as a disco ball). Like the hippies, drugs became an important part of the experience as well: many clubs were notorious for cocaine abuse and distribution. At the beginning of the trend, discos prided themselves on being open and welcoming to people of all backgrounds, but as the 1970s came to an end, exclusivity helped add to a club's allure.

Discos often featured elaborate light effects to enhance the dancers' experiences, and they usually featured a mirrored "disco ball" like this one.

How Disco Sounds

Disco's ultimate goal is to provide a solid, danceable beat. Disco artists use a diverse lineup of techniques to create their own particular brand, but many characteristics are considered standard. The bass line, typically played by the bass guitar and bass drum, is essential. While the drum beats a steady **four-on-the-floor**, meaning that it plays consistently on every single beat, the bass guitar (or sometimes a bass line played by an electric piano) plays a heavily syncopated rhythm, at direct odds with the drum. Keeping the drum on a simple rhythm allows dancers to easily hear the beat and feel when to move, but emphasizing weak beats with another low voice gives the music a dense, exotic polyrhythmic sound. Another standard character-istic of disco is its use of electronic instruments, often including synthesizers of some kind. Many artists make use of electronic drum kits or even drum modules, which synthesize a number of drum sounds and rhythmic effects.

Another interesting twist that disco featured was the use of instruments typical to the orchestra. Orchestral string and woodwind instruments like violins, violas, cellos, and flutes had long been absent from popular music, but they took the lead in a number of popular disco tracks. Electric guitar was an essential element to rock melodies, but in disco it was either relegated to a minor rhythmic element or left out altogether.

The vocals featured in disco are a direct contrast to the styles popular in rock at the time. As previously mentioned, rock in the 1970s was largely geared toward and performed by white men at the time. Disco dis-tinctly went out of its way to feature different voices: black female vocalists with heavy gospel-inspired style are some of disco's biggest divas (Thelma Houston, Gloria Gaynor, and Donna Summer all sang gospel in their early careers and provided some of the biggest disco hits of all time). Other styles became popular in the later

The Bee Gees, brothers Maurice, Robin, and Barry Gibb, hit their stride at the height of the disco trend. Their falsetto voices provided a sharp contrast to the lower, gravelly voices popular in the day's rock.

years of disco, like Diana Ross's smooth Motown sound and higher, softer male vocals like Barry and Robin Gibb of the Bee Gees. Some later disco tracks like Sugarhill Gang's "Rapper's Delight" even served as the first examples of hip-hop and rap heard nationwide. Disco vocals were often emotionally stirring, but disco lyrics lacked the poetic depth and political symbolism of rock lyrics at the time. Disco's main goal wasn't political protest or social progress: it simply existed to make people dance. It was an escape for a generation that was war-weary and social groups that simply wanted to belong. Disco was musically innovative, lyrically innocuous, and impossibly catchy.

The Height of Disco

When the early 1970s rolled around, disco was already a mainstay in urban dance clubs. It wasn't until 1973 that the first few disco tracks like Love Unlimited Orchestra's "Love's Theme" and MFSB's "The Sound of Philadelphia" began to top the Billboard Hot 100. By 1974, disco wasn't just for dancing in dark clubs anymore, it was now a viable and widely marketable genre. Trends in American popular culture began to emulate the fashion, music, and dance moves of the typical disco patron. By 1975, every major city in America had at least one well-known, exclusive disco: Los Angeles had Studio One, Atlanta had The Library, and until 1977, Leviticus was the hottest disco in New York. In April of that year, however, a new club opened and attracted more attention than the others combined. **Studio 54**'s grand opening on the night of Tuesday, April 26th was a bit grander than planned: 1,500 invitations had been sent out, but 4,000 guests arrived. The venue's popularity would only grow from there.

Studio 54 catered to Hollywood stars (Cher attended the opening and regularly after that) and the artistic elite in New York (Andy Warhol was also a regular fixture). The building was originally a television studio, so the space was easily rigged with new lighting fixtures, televisions to display graphics, and fly systems to create an all-encompassing, theatrical experience for the revelers. Though discos were named for their usage of records or "discs" in lieu of live acts, Studio 54 hosted some of the hottest bands and singers of the time. Stevie Wonder and James Brown were some of the earliest mainstream artists to perform at the Studio 54, but the club also launched the careers of new disco-focused artists, like Sylvester and The Village People.

Disco-themed movies and merchandise capitalized on the trend, but also led to its eventual market saturation and downfall.

Throughout the rest of 1977, disco continued its reign at the top of American popular culture. Billboard's Hot 100 was filled with disco hits like Thelma Houston's "Don't Leave Me This Way," Andy Gibb's "I Just Want to Be Your Everything," and The Emotions' "Best of My Love." The genre broke through in the biggest way yet in December of that year when the film "Saturday Night Fever" was released. The film told a very recognizable story for audiences of the time: a young man, lacking direction and a stable career, uses his local disco as an escape from his frustrating daily life. The movie received decent reviews, but it is best remembered for its remarkable soundtrack, which prominently featured the Bee Gees and rocketed them to fame shortly afterward.

Disco's Decline

Disco followed the pattern of many trends before it: it began as part of an underground counterculture movement, and then it was adopted by young people as a means of escape and expression. Later, it became a highly popular style that as many artists emulated as possible in an effort to be "on-trend." Then, it became the pinnacle of popular culture, inspiring movies, television programs, books, and fashion. At the end, disco faced the same fate: it became a diluted, tiresome version of its former self that was only recognizable in its contributions to newer genres and styles.

For the hippies, their climax came in 1967 and the movement faded away after pop culture had drained it dry. The same moment came for disco in 1979. There had long been an anti-disco sentiment in rock culture, as rock musicians and fans considered disco devoid of true expression and emotion. "Disco Sucks" shirts were popular among rock fans, and whenever a popular rock artist would incorporate disco elements into a new song, hardline rock fans turned their backs on them and deemed them inauthentic. On July 12, 1979, at a Chicago White Sox game, fans were given discounted tickets if they brought a disco record to be destroyed at what they called "Disco Demolition Night." About 48,000 people attended, and when the disco records were piled up to be destroyed, 7,000 disco haters stormed the field to participate in the destruction.

Though this one event wasn't the only thing to cause the fall of disco, it was symptomatic of the nation's feelings toward it in general. Studio 54 closed its doors in February of 1980 and though it would later reopen, it would never again have the same status it once held. Disco artists were finding it hard to stay on the charts: by the end of 1979, there were few disco hits topping Billboard's Hot 100 chart, save for Chic's "Good Times" and Michael Jackson's "Rock with You" (which topped the R&B charts as well, providing an argument that it's not truly a "disco" song).

Some disco musical elements, like the "four-on-the-floor" bass drum beat and gospel vocals, continued to live on in the popular music of the 1980s. Disco's prominent use of electronic instruments and production techniques would prove incredibly popular in the New Wave, dance, and pop music of the 1980s as well. Other sounds, like the use of orchestral instruments, became passé and faded away with the rest of the movement. In today's music, disco musical elements are often used as a kitschy throwback device, though it's partly because of disco's influence that most popular music is heavily edited electronically and not just performed by live instruments.

CHAPTER FIVE

Hard Rock, Punk, and New Wave in the 1970s and 1980s

Like the hippies of the previous decade, some young people in the 1970s turned to communal music as a way to express their frustration with the system and their feelings of powerlessness against it. Unlike the hippies, however, these young people didn't feel the need to express their dissent in a peaceful, humble way. They were angry, they were loud, and they needed music that would communicate that as directly as possible.

Rock Coming into the 1970s

Jimi Hendrix's performance at the Monterey Pop Festival in 1967 was the first time a large American audience was introduced to the fuzzy, gritty sound of distortion and feedback in an electric guitar. Hendrix used the effect to create what he felt was a more real, unpolished, harder sound. Others caught on and referred to this trend as **hard rock**. The first hard rock singles to top the Billboard Hot 100 appeared in 1973 and 1974, with Grand Funk's "We're an American Band" and Bachman Turner Overdrive's "You Ain't Seen Nothing Yet," respectively. The turn toward a darker, harder sound was a response to the tumultuous nature of the decade and represented a need to create something rough and unpolished. Disco was too commercial and its lyrics too shallow; hard rock was grounded, raw, and emotional.

Shock Rock and Glam Rock

Hard rock continued to grow in popularity throughout the 1970s, and it began to branch into a number of sub-genres. **Shock rock** used the basic sound of early hard rock, but with an edgier presentation and more shocking lyrics. Alice Cooper was a pioneer in shocking audiences at his shows, incorporating fake blood and violence. He released his album *School's Out* in 1972 and, through provocative in lyrics and performance, it struck a serious chord with mainstream audiences. The Stooges and their lead singer Iggy Pop pushed the envelope in a similar way, smearing themselves with raw hamburger or sometimes engaging in self-mutilation on stage. Doubling down on Cooper and Pop's theatricality, hard rock band Kiss rose to prominence in 1975 by wearing elaborate makeup and costumes, incorporating several pyrotechnic tricks and spitting fake blood during their concerts.

Other bands still admired the entertainment value of shock rock, but didn't like the gore. Makeup, pyrotechnics, and elaborate costumes, along with showy vocals and ostentatious guitar solos were the bedrock of the trend known as **glam rock** (short for "glamorous"). The name captured what these groups aimed to be: a visually glamorous, extravagant version of hard rock that also showcased the band's talents.

Queen

One of the most influential rock bands of the 1970s was **Queen**, whose style can't truly be captured by the simple descriptor of "glam." Queen certainly had the glam rock sound, but their influences were wide and varied, so their music was as well. The band formed in 1971 and featured a young man named Farrokh Bulsara on lead vocals. Bulsara had a flamboyant, flashy onstage persona and decided a stage name would better suit him; he settled on the name "Freddie Mercury." Brian May, John Deacon, and Roger Taylor made up the rest of the band. The four young men were all stellar musicians and songwriters in their own right: each member is credited for writing at least one number one hit for the group. They took care that each member of the band was equally celebrated and able to express their individual style.

Queen was first signed to EMI in 1973 and released their first studio album that year. It garnered a bit of buzz, but it wasn't until 1975 that the band truly reached worldwide superstardom with the release of their album *A Night at the Opera*. The album title hinted at the theatricality of the songs within—one of which was "Bohemian Rhapsody." At 5:55 long, the song is far longer than the typical radio hit. Not only that, but it was written without a recognizable song form—in other words, it is through-composed. The song vacillates back and forth between slow piano harmonies and high-energy guitar-driven climaxes. It is even widely credited as the first song with an accompanying music video, a concept that many artists would emulate afterward to promote their own work. Its popularity, along with several other tracks on the album, led to *A Night at the Opera* being certified Platinum by the RIAA.

© marekusz/Shutterstock.com

A statue of Queen lead singer Freddie Mercury stands in Montreux, Switzerland.

The following year, the group released a double single, titled "We Will Rock You" and "We Are the Champions." 1979 brought the hit single "Crazy Little Thing Called Love." In 1980, the band released "Another One Bites the Dust," which would become their highest-selling American single, and they even wrote the soundtrack for the movie *Flash Gordon*. The group continued to tour and perform throughout the 1980s, though their 1970s work remains some of their most enduring. In 1991, Freddie Mercury was one of the first world-famous musicians to announce that he had AIDS; he died the day after he made the announcement.

Queen made a number of strong musical choices that innovated and changed music in the 1970s and 1980s. Bohemian Rhapsody's music video gave other artists the idea to use the same promotional tactic, and eventually led to the development of MTV in 1981. The group's fashion choices, including a heavy use of drag clothing and makeup, inspired many more groups to experiment with flamboyant and glamorous styles to wow their audiences. Musically, all members were virtuosos in their respective instruments; Freddie Mercury even recorded a theme song for the 1992 Summer Olympics in Barcelona with renowned opera singer Montserrat Caballé. The group's flare for theatrics, inventive promotional tactics, and formidable musical talent have inspired many rock groups that have come to follow them.

Punk

Even though it was considered more "real" than the rest of popular music at the time, there were many who disliked seeing hard rock "sell out" and go glam or mainstream. Though it was significantly rougher and more distorted than the typical rock they'd grown up on, it was becoming more commonplace and had lost its rebellious edge. It no longer spoke to their concerns and feelings. Burdened by a rough economy providing very little

© Corky Buczyk/Shutterstock.com

New York City's CBGB club, home to some of the earliest and most iconic punk performances in the 1970s.

hope for the future, they wanted to feel free and reckless instead of hopeless and scared. This sentiment gave birth to the sound of **punk rock**.

Rock had been the music of rebels since its inception, but young people who grew up on it considered its original rough edges to be rather soft by now. The simple sound of drums, electric guitar, bass, and voice set to common time had been so thoroughly explored by the mid-1970s that there was very little left to do with it. Young amateurs played together in their garages and dreamed up new sounds. These "garage bands" took the simple rock template and extended it into the avant-garde: faster tempos, shouted or screamed vocals, and deliberate guitar feedback challenged the audience rather than catering to them. Most early punk acts were considered unmarketable by record companies because of their incredibly rough and deliberately ugly sound. Punk bands prided themselves on being shut off from the mainstream. Punk was considered a means of raw expression, free from the need to sell records or make money. The more unpolished and unrehearsed a band sounded, the more integrity they maintained in the punk scene.

In the United States, New York was the center of early punk. CBGB, a club in lower Manhattan, showcased the early stars of the punk movement, namely Television and Patti Smith. This is where the typical punk clothing style developed: ripped clothing, leather jackets with studs, and messy hair communicated the rough edge and apathy that drove the movement. In the United Kingdom, London was the center of the first stirrings of the punk scene.

Different punk bands had different messages and aims with their music and performances. Television, a seminal band in the New York scene, was much more organized and musically proficient than others, drawing on a wide variety of influences and attempting to create avant-garde rock rather than chaotic punk. Patti Smith aimed to agitate crowds with her poetic lyrics. The Ramones had a more tongue-in-cheek approach, with an upbeat, dirtier version of pop-influenced punk. On the other side of the Atlantic, London artists explored a number of styles as well. The Sex Pistols were one of the more deliberately defiant and outrageous acts: they made several unfavorable references to the British monarchy and their performances often whipped audiences into violent chaos. The Clash were also quite politically subversive, but in a more organized way: many of their songs advocated for far-left political policies and, like Television in the United States, the group experimented with a number of rock styles. Siouxsie and the Banshees experimented with punk sounds at first, but later evolved into a more polished new wave sound. Regardless of the approach, the heart of punk was the draw of the untested, the unpolished, and the uncharted.

Punk eventually died down in the late 1970s, but its influence was felt going into the 1980s as new waves of sound were coming about. Darker variants emerged, like gothic rock and industrial music. Pop artists, like Madonna, later appropriated elements of punk fashion. Though it was heavily adopted by the mainstream going into the 1980s, the trend of young people innovating for the purposes of artistic expression rather than commercialism was revived in the Grunge of the early 1990s and the Emo and Garage rock trends of the early 2000s.

New Wave

The term new wave to refer to music was originally interchangeable with "punk" when it first started appearing in the early 1970s. As the punk trend died down and many of its musical characteristics filtered into new genres, **new wave** came to mean a more upbeat, electronically mixed, "poppy" version of punk. In 1979, Blondie had its first number one hit with "Heart of Glass." The band was originally considered a punk group and had even played at CBGB in its heyday, but had since adopted a smoother, more commercial sound with synthesizers and pop-oriented vocals that typified the new wave sound.

Later that year, The Knack's "My Sharona" also topped the charts while using the same musical ingredients as punk: distorted guitar, heavy percussion, and a rough, punk-style vocal. The difference was in the organization: rather than a loud drone, the guitar played a cheeky staccato melody and later a virtuosic solo. The vocals incorporated clean, close harmonies. The percussion built up to a forte at times, but pulled back to make way for other musical elements to come through. Blondie and The Knack typified the early new wave movement: artists who borrowed heavily from punk, but cleaned up the sound to be more marketable and more expressive.

Blondie lead singer Debbie Harry led the group out of their punk beginnings and into their next phase as new wave artists.

Many new wave bands even made use of the synthesizers popular on disco tracks—where punk was about innovation for the sake of eschewing the establishment, new wave was about creating new sounds that challenged and intrigued listeners.

As the 1970s drew to a close and the 1980s began, rock had grown into several vast and diverse genres. Psychedelic and acid rock had given way to punk, which then trickled down into the many definitions of new wave. Popular music drew from far more influences now than it ever had: a single pop song might feature a disco-inspired synthesizer, a gospel vocal, and punk-derived power chords all at the same time. Musicians were free to call upon as many styles as necessary to create their own unique sound.

The Development of Rap and Its Beginnings in the 1970s and 1980s

Though the upscale discos of the 1970s had closed by the end of the decade, the trend of dancing to prerecorded music mixed by a DJ was still incredibly popular at neighborhood block parties in predominantly black and Latino communities. Rap and hip hop culture grew out of these trends. Though it's often viewed as a relatively "new" genre, rap borrows from much older musical traditions, some going back hundreds of years. In general, **rap** is recognized as spoken, rhymed lyrics delivered rhythmically over an instrumental background accompaniment. Several factors influence the overall style of each rap artist: rhythmic delivery style and rhyme scheme or "flow," lyrical content and delivery, and instrumental accompaniment. The prevailing style since the late 1970s has been to deliver lyrics over an electronically produced accompaniment or **instrumental**. Typically, these instrumentals make use of **sampling**, a technique by which a portion of a preexisting song (sometimes as long as an entire verse or chorus, or as short as a two-beat portion of a riff) is mixed with other layers to produce a new instrumental. Different trends in flow, instrumentals, and content have come and gone over the past forty years or so of rap's prevalence, with new artists innovating constantly.

Rap's Earliest Roots

The roots of what could first be recognized as rap developed with the West African *Jaliyaa* tradition (also referred to as *Griot* tradition). *Jaliyaa* was an important spoken art form in several West African cultures, in which a speaker, known as a *Jali* (for males) or *Jalimuso* (for females), delivered rhythmic speeches about history, local news, or general goings on of the village. The jali and jalimusoare rather similar to the troubadour and minstrel of European culture in their function: both served as important channels for news and information. However, Jaliyaa was spoken, not sung, and only used musical accompaniment in some instances. Troubadours and minstrels typically focused on writing melodies that matched the emotional or informational content of their stories, but jalolu (plural of jali) were much more concerned with innovating new rhythmic structures to add interest and depth. As jaliyaa tradition existed in many of the tribes from which people were abducted for the transatlantic slave trade, the style persisted as a link to their home cultures. It even made its way into song forms used by later generations of slaves, including work songs, religious hymns, and coded songs with instructions to escape.

The rhythmic style of jaliyaa tradition is most clearly found in the twentieth century beginning with early blues bands. Before the adoption of electric instruments to play the blues, **jug bands** were wildly popular in rural areas and anywhere most musicians didn't have access to electric guitars or expensive brass instruments. Jugs, washboards, and spoons took the place of formal instruments to keep steady beats and accompany a vocalist who told a story. Often, instead of singing, the vocalist would simply speak rhythmically over the band, much like the jalolu, to play around with different dramatic effects. Though this type of vocal delivery didn't catch on nationally, it remained popular in small pockets of African American fans of live music.

Few performers recorded in this spoken style so early, so it's hard to track the development of the sound. Still, gems like John Lee Hooker's "Boogie Chillen," recorded in 1948, give an idea of how spoken lyrics were used as a storytelling device. Hooker played a simple guitar riff and alternated sung verses with rhythmically spoken verses in order to amplify the drama of the story. The song's simple components of a continuously repeated riff for accompaniment, lyrics delivered in time over the music, and an occasionally sung or pitched vocal delivery became core to what would essentially shape itself into rap later in the century.

Hip Hop Culture

Throughout the 1970s, as discos thrived in trendy and expensive neighborhoods, residents in lower-income neighborhoods found their own way to let loose and dance at block parties. Residents of a city block closed off a portion of the road and set up sound systems with speakers, record turntables, and microphones. Usually the setup would feature at least two record turntables, to allow for a seamless transition between songs. The microphone was used as a way to make announcements to the crowd over the music and conversation.

Song selection and announcements were left up to the disc jockey or DJ. DJs made an art of transitioning between songs, sometimes repeating certain portions of the previous song over the beginning of the next. It was also popular to use **scratching**, the sound of the turntable needle scratching a record, as a musical effect to give the continuous music a little more of an interactive and live feel. Later, DJs began playing around with new ways to deliver their announcements by rhyming their words and making them work rhythmically with the music playing over the speakers.

In the later 1970s, the influx of Caribbean immigrants (specifically those from Jamaica) to New York meant that their traditions worked their way into the city's block parties. Jamaican immigrants brought **toasting** with them—a form of delivering spoken, rhymed monologue over music or percussive beats (a Jamaican interpretation of the jaliyaa tradition). Many block parties in New York started featuring both a DJ who selected or mixed music and another performer who would make verbal announcements and perform Jamaican-style toasts, known as a **rapper**. The name hip hop is said to have originated in one of these rap toasts: Keith "Cowboy" Wiggins first used it to refer to military marching (while giving his friend Kokomo a hard time about joining the Army and learning to march in line). Eventually, Cowboy and fellow rapper Lovebug Starski developed it into a tongue-twisting break between sets of written lyrics. The term "hip hop" stuck, as it was representative of not

DJs often had more than one turntable at a time to transition seamlessly between songs.

only the rhythmic nature of the music but also the spontaneous feel of the vocal delivery. Starski and Cowboy's delivery of the original "hip hop" routine never made wide circulation, but Wonder Mike of the Sugarhill Gang used it as the opening portion of his verse on the song "Rapper's Delight."

The term **hip hop** came to eventually represent all aspects of the culture, not just the vocal component. Break dancers and graffiti artists were considered important members of hip hop culture as well. The style transitioned from outdoor block parties to indoor concert venues, and DJs began mixing and recording lyric-free tracks from existing records to accommodate the rappers with whom they often worked. Rappers would entertain crowds by rhyming lyrics over these tracks, usually speaking of their own talent, their neighborhood or hometown, or the event at which they were performing. Hip hop was its own musical genre at this point, and its early stars carved out their own particular brands of it.

Grandmaster Flash and the Furious Five

Not only one of the earliest popular recording acts of the genre, Grandmaster Flash and the Furious Five also pioneered much of the early hip hop vernacular. The group consisted of DJ Grandmaster Flash and five rappers he frequently worked with: Cowboy (who, as mentioned above, originated the term "hip hop"), Melle Mel (who was the first rapper to refer to himself as an **MC**, short for "master of ceremonies"), Kidd Creole, Rahiem, and Scorpio.

Grandmaster Flash's family was a part of the wave of Caribbean immigrants to New York City in the 1970s; his Barbadian family settled in the Bronx. He grew up with a diverse collection of neighbors from other immigrant cultures, and block parties were a big part of his childhood. His mother encouraged him to tinker around

Four of the original "Furious Five": Scorpio, Melle Mel (who later changed his name to "Mele Mel"), Kidd Creole, and Rahiem.

with electronics and his father had amassed a huge record collection. The combination of these two influences led to his development as an accomplished DJ and sampler. Eventually, he formed the Furious Five and performed with the group at concerts and parties. The group became so well-known that they were even invited to perform at discos, which was quite rare for hip hop groups at the time. Eventually, they earned a record deal with Sugarhill Records and began to be recognized by mainstream audiences.

Perhaps the most influential single by the group was their 1982 release "The Message." Despite the prevalence of party-style raps, where MCs rhymed largely about their own talent and popularity, "The Message" went in an entirely different direction. Melle Mel is the primary rapper on the track, alongside guest rapper Duke Bootee, and the two of them speak frankly about the difficulties of life as a young person yearning to break out of inner-city poverty. The track underneath the lyrics incorporates a number of electronic effects and riffs that have been widely sampled in later hip hop instrumentals. The raw nature of the lyrics and their strong delivery by Melle Mel are what many consider to be a turning point for hip hop: prior to this, rappers had been sidekicks to DJs, who had always been the bigger stars. "The Message" became iconic for its lyrical content. It became a source of inspiration for later DJs who sampled its sound, and an example for young rappers who wanted to make a name for themselves in the new, national hip hop movement.

The New School and Gangster Rap

Beginning in the early 1980s, as hip hop became popular in the mainstream, many rappers tried to distance themselves from the commercial aspect of the industry in a number of ways. These anti-commercial rappers became incorporated into what was called the "new school" in the mid-1980s. Many of these rappers identified with the rough life Melle Mel and Duke Bootee spoke of on "The Message" and focused on adopting a "tougher" attitude and more rhythmically innovative sound to go with it. Their lyrical content was much more provocative as well, borrowing from the bravado of party rap toasts and doubling down on Melle Mel's social commentary. Others in the "new school" focused instead on expanding creatively, sampling from as wide a variety of genres as possible and rapping about history, philosophy, and interpersonal relationships.

One of the most influential groups in this latter category was De La Soul, who formed in 1987 in New York. Their first studio album, *3 Feet High and Rising*, established them as important members of the new hip hop class. The album's lead single, "Me Myself and I," borrows heavily from the sounds of "old school" instrumentals with samples from funk songs and synthesized riffs, but it also incorporates the popular drum machine sound and subtler lyric delivery popular in the new school. Overall, it evokes the same upbeat mood of the party rap of the previous generation but with lyrics that are emotionally honest, socially aware, and philosophically oriented.

On the other side of the spectrum, groups like Public Enemy and NWA, both formed in 1986, typically gravitated toward the harder edge of hip hop. Their style became known as **gangster rap** for its association with gang activity and violence. Their lyrics were brutally honest about the realities of life for urban youth: lyrics about police brutality, drug use, and gang activity were typical, as was near-constant profanity. Their instrumentals usually had a harder edge as well: NWA's single "Straight Outta Compton" from the album of the same name incorporates live drums layered over a drum machine, as well as a looped horn riff that ends up sounding like an ominous drone.

Both of these newer styles found dedicated audiences. While De La Soul's more poetic sound had obvious crossover appeal, surprisingly, it was gangster rap that sold better in the long run. NWA's album *Straight Outta Compton* was one of the first albums released with a "Parental Advisory" warning, and many singles from the album were banned from mainstream radio play due to the violent nature and profane content of the lyrics. Many parents and politicians denounced the album for its offensive content and language, but this only served to fuel curiosity and rebellion. Suburban teens with no connection whatsoever to gang culture in Los Angeles flocked to music stores to buy the album, often without their parents' knowledge. Ultimately, by sparking controversy, NWA started a conversation. Their lyrics, though rough, brought to life the realities for millions of

Posdnuos (Kelvin Mercer) of De La Soul at a concert in 2017. Though the band hit their stride in the 1980s and 1990s, their socially aware brand of hip hop continues to draw crowds.

Americans living with poverty, police brutality, and institutionalized racism in the late 1980s and early 1990s. The album now has a staggering legacy: it has sold three million copies to date and was the first hip hop album to garner a five-star rating from Rolling Stone.

We'll discuss the effects of hip hop's rise in later chapters as we take a look at the last few decades of music, but it's been a strong force in shaping all genres of popular music since its inception.

By 1980, artists began to see the advantages of not identifying too strongly with one genre over another. The most legendary were those who combined a number of influences and carved out their own unique style. Disco was mostly dead, but its use of synthesizers and electronic mixing software were found in both hip hop and bubblegum pop. Punk was no longer in its heyday, but new wave music incorporated many of its experimental sounds and individualist sentiments. Motown artists like Michael Jackson and Stevie Wonder branched out from their roots and dabbled in disco, funk, and rock. Experimentation and freedom were the name of the game—within certain limits. The image of being an individual was highly prized, without being too off-putting in terms of sound. In fact, an artist's image became especially important as the music industry encountered a huge change in 1981 that shifted the focus off of sound.

MTV and the Rise of the Music Video

MTV aired its first music video on August 1, 1981. The channel aimed to offer an enhancement to what radio had done for about 50 years: rather than simply playing songs by popular artists, now viewers could actually watch their favorite bands perform in music videos. Music videos are short films constructed around the concept of a song, and are often used to promote the song and the artist. The first music videos were just video recordings of a band or an artist performing live, but soon these simple performance videos were replaced with high-concept stories that starred the recording artist. Record companies provided music videos for free to MTV as a promotional tool, so the channel's business model was incredibly lucrative. Hosts, known as **VJs** (**video jockeys**, a play on the term "disc jockeys"), would introduce blocks of videos and interview bands on the air.

Teens had long relied on their favorite radio stations to introduce them to the newest songs and artists, but the audiovisual hook of MTV blew radio out of the water. Artists with more visual appeal (more attractive looks, eye-catching style, or impressive dance moves) used the new art form to their advantage. Glam rock, new wave, and heavy metal bands were especially popular in early MTV rotation. Glam rock and heavy metal bands recreated their live performances with dramatic costumes, pyrotechnics, and wild stage antics. New wave acts featured quirky visual effects and stories based upon their songs. Many artists caught onto the importance of the music video early and used it as a way to set themselves apart not just as musicians, but as multifaceted artists. Michael Jackson and Madonna were some of the earliest hit-makers on MTV, and both used the platform in different ways to launch different portions of their careers.

Michael Jackson

Though most young people know **Michael Jackson** for his career high in the 1980s, he began his music career in 1969 as the lead singer of The Jackson 5 at age 11. The band signed with Motown Records and released several soul and pop hits in the early 1970s. Jackson's strong vocals and stage presence made him the clear standout of the group, and after releasing a few solo singles on his own, he officially left the band in 1975. The late 1970s were a time a growth for Jackson: he starred as the Scarecrow in *The Wiz*, and collaborated with renowned music producer Quincy Jones on his 1979 album *Off the Wall*.

By the time MTV debuted in 1981, Jackson was already setting records in music and proving himself as a cross-genre pioneer. Jackson fit the MTV star mold perfectly: he was attractive, a skilled dancer, and had a flair for creating compelling stories. MTV debuted the music video for Jackson's single "Billie Jean" in 1983. The video was a huge success for both parties. MTV attracted a wider, more diverse audience, and Jackson realized the potential of the new medium to express his creative skill. He began to think even bigger, with ideas of expanding his next videos to feature more complex storylines, spoken dialogue, and more characters. Later that year, he proved his mastery of the art form with the music video for his single "Thriller."

Michael Jackson's unique style and flair for visual drama made him the biggest star of the 1980s.

© Vicki L. Miller/Shutterstock.com

Thriller

The eponymous hit from his 1982 album "Thriller" was originally a romantic song titled "Starlight." In the original lyrics, Jackson sings about love and "starlight" bringing him and his love interest together. He wasn't entirely sold on this concept, however. Jackson, producer Quincy Jones, and songwriter Rod Temperton eventually came up with a novel idea: make an homage to horror movies, and use Jackson's popularity on MTV to launch a horror-themed music video for the song. Horror-themed songs had seen some success as novelties in the past (Bobby Pickett's "Monster Mash" as possibly the most famous example), but Jackson and his team hoped to make a mainstream hit out of the offbeat concept. The team reworked the lyrics to be about a spooky night, added a voiceover by horror legend Vincent Price, and added creepy sound effects to help tell the story. To launch the single, Jackson hired film director John Landis and choreographer Michael Peters and the team designed a fourteen-minute music video. Thriller debuted on MTV on December 2, 1983, and was a staple for the channel for years afterward. For the first time, music videos were viewed as more than promotional tools. Thriller proved they could stand alone as pieces of art.

Thriller, the album, was a career high for Jackson, due in part to the success of its associated music videos. Jackson's next album, *Bad*, was nearly as successful and produced a crop of innovative music videos as well. (That album's lead single, "Bad," had a corresponding music video that was nearly three minutes longer than Thriller.) Jackson continued to churn out top hits throughout the 1980s, though his popularity waned some in the 1990s. He lost some endorsement deals due to painkiller addiction, and lost popular favor due to accusations of child molestation. Regardless of the difficulties in his private life, Michael Jackson was a celebrated artist and pioneer of pop music up until his death in 2009.

Madonna

Another breakout star of the MTV era was Madonna Ciccone, who adopted her first name as her stage name. **Madonna** grew up in Michigan, but established herself as a dancer and singer on the New York scene in the early 1980s. Madonna's dancing skills, outrageous style, and love of controversy were the perfect combination to gain some serious attention in the new popular music video format. Her first album, *Madonna*, produced a few Billboard hits and music videos. It wasn't until she debuted her second album, *Like a Virgin*, that she truly began to push the limits of the music video and MTV's visual format. Her video for the album's eponymous single featured alternate scenes of Madonna dancing provocatively, and then looking chaste in a wedding dress. Her performance of the song at MTV's Video Music Awards in 1984 was one of the most iconic and controversial of her career: dressed in a wedding dress, she writhed on stage and simulated sex acts. Madonna caught on early to the advantage MTV provided: her music only did so much to catch her audience's attention, but their visual components (music videos and live performances) could go even further. Her music video for the song "Material Girl" was just as visually captivating, with Madonna recreating a scene performed by Marilyn Monroe in the film *Gentlemen Prefer Blondes*. Madonna created her own image as a new sex symbol by paying homage to those who came before her and pushing the envelope in her own new, provocative way.

Like a Prayer

By the late 1980s, Madonna had cemented her place as a pop star with her clever image manipulation. She recognized, however, that other stars on MTV tended to fade away once the public had tired of their persona. Madonna became a master of inventing new looks, new sounds, and new controversy to stay relevant. In 1989, she released her fourth album *Like a Prayer*. The lead single, also titled "Like a Prayer," featured lyrics heavy with religious symbolism and gospel-style backup vocals. When its music video debuted, it was unlike anything seen on the network before. The song's religious aspects were exaggerated for its visual component: scenes from the video featured Madonna wearing a revealing dress while dancing in front of burning crosses, experiencing stigmata, and kissing an actor portraying a saint. The juxtaposition of erotic and Catholic imagery outraged religious groups who demanded a boycott of the singer's single, album, and concert tour. The video was supposed to coincide with a new ad campaign for Pepsi starring Madonna, but due to public outcry she was quickly dropped. Madonna was likely aware of the controversy the video would bring, but released it anyway. This became a part of her business model—when she was deemed too edgy or controversial, it only generated more attention and record sales. Indeed, the record boycott worked in her favor: *Like a Prayer* is her longest-running number one album as of 2018, having spent six weeks at the top of the charts. Many artists to follow have copied the "controversy sells" technique, but none have mastered it quite the way that Madonna did.

Madonna continues to tour and record extensively, and her albums continue to top the charts nearly 40 years after her debut.

Madonna pursued a number of other artistic outlets in the 1990s: she earned a Golden Globe for Best Actress in 1996 for her role in *Evita* and started her own entertainment company and record label in 1992. She has continued to produce top-selling albums well into the new millennium, constantly reinventing her sound and style to keep her approach fresh and her fans riveted.

Popular Music of the 1980s

The biggest trend that carried over from the 1970s into the 1980s was the use of synthesizers to create instrumental tracks in popular music. Synthesizers had been used in music production for decades, but their first prominent use in pop music was in the new wave trend of the late 1970s. Where traditional instruments could only produce a narrow range of predictable sounds, synthesizers captured the unorthodox edge that new wave gained from punk and allowed artists to play with new ideas and sounds. The use of synthesizers in pop music was particularly popular with European bands in the early 1980s, but British **synth-pop** (a widely appealing brand of new wave that embraced a pop sound and heavy synthesizers) bands like Duran Duran, the Human League, and Spandau Ballet introduced the trend to American audiences, and eventually American artists as well. Most subgenres of 1980s pop experimented with synthesized instrumentals from time to time.

Rock and roll continued on its trend toward the heavier, grittier edge of metal. The distorted rhythm guitars, prominent drums, and virtuosic solos of metal had been popular since the early 1970s, but they became com-

Duran Duran's sound has evolved over time, but their 1980s style is quintessential synth-pop.

monplace in the rock and roll of the 1980s. The "glam" image of bands like Queen in the 1970s also became a template for the new metal bands of the 1980s. A number of subgenres (with quite a bit of crossover) grew out of the glam trend. **Hair metal** was a tongue-in-cheek name for the style of music played by bands with excessively styled hair and outfits. **Arena rock** referred to the style of music played by bands who toured in large venues and incorporated a number of visual components (light shows, pyrotechnics) into their performances. Prominent metal bands like Motley Crue, Guns N' Roses, and Poison sold tens of thousands of tickets per concert and millions of albums worldwide. This commercialism confirmed that metal had lost its genuine rebellious edge, but still played at it with suggestive lyrics and wild on-stage antics.

Though hip hop was still a relatively young genre in the 1980s, it was diversifying quickly. Rap vocals were featured on a number of pop and rock tracks, most prominently on Run DMC and Aerosmith's "Walk This Way." Hip hop songs from producers like Grandmaster Flash attracted fans in their own right (and had a large part in popularizing synthesized instrumentals). Another important development was a style known as **New Jack Swing**. Hip hop producers created the distinct new style by combining synthesized drum beats (specifically with the Roland TR-808 **drum machine**), sampled instrumental hits, and R&B vocals for an upbeat new dance style that was particularly popular in New York dance clubs. Janet Jackson's song "Nasty" is one of its earliest appearances, and New Edition's early work is a nostalgic revival of 1960s bubblegum pop-style vocals with new jack swing instrumentation.

Though the 1980s was a high point for the use of the synthesizer, it also saw the rebirth of classic **country music**. The soundtrack to the 1980 film *Urban Cowboy* featured a number of pop-country tracks, many of which became top sellers that year. This sparked a revival of country style among wider audiences. Kenny Rogers

Janet Jackson was a pioneer in New Jack Swing in the 1980s.

and Dolly Parton, both country icons in the 1970s, enjoyed mainstream success with several high-charting hits. Toward the end of the 1980s, the "pop" element of pop-country was fading out and more country artists drew on the genre's roots: steel guitar, banjo, and mandolin were featured more prominently, and bluegrass- and folk-style vocals overtook the pop-rock style of the early 1980s.

Grunge, Divas, and the Golden Age of Hip Hop in the 1990s

In the 1980s, MTV revolutionized pop culture by popularizing the music video. Suddenly, the visual component of music was just as important to an artist's appeal as their sound. Though this remained true throughout the 1990s, there were a number of changes that set the two decades apart drastically.

Grunge and Alternative Rock

1980s rock was a combination of metal and glam trends of the 1970s, with an emphasis on big crowds, big sounds, and big hair. This was largely gone by the early 1990s, when rock fans yearned for a less-polished, antiestablishment sound reminiscent of punk. **Grunge** kept metal's distorted electric guitar sound and heavy, insistent drum sound. The grunge-style vocal was a raspier, lower-pitched version of the higher metal "scream." While metal guitar solos tended to show off the guitarist's skill with a quick flurry of notes and virtuosic improvisation, guitar solos in grunge were more understated, echoing the main melody. Grunge lyrics were darker and more socially conscious than metal, focusing on topics like depression, relationships, and commercialism.

Nirvana

One of the most popular grunge bands was **Nirvana**. Lead singer Kurt Cobain, drummer Dave Grohl, and bassist Krist Novoselic began on the underground rock scene in Seattle, and were eventually signed by DGC Records. (DGC Records would later sign a number of influential alternative rock bands and artists like Beck, Weezer, and Sonic Youth.) Nirvana's first breakthrough hit was "Smells Like Teen Spirit," the first single from their album *Nevermind*. The song became an overnight favorite on college rock radio stations and eventually made its way onto alternative rock stations in major markets. Cobain had mixed feelings about the group's success, and even obscured his face in the song's now iconic music video. After the band had a string of top hits on Billboard's Alternative charts (and a few in the Hot 100), Kurt Cobain eventually committed suicide on April 5, 1994. Grunge had already begun to fall out of popularity, but Cobain's death was particularly detrimental to the genre. By about 1995, grunge elements like the lower vocal, more subdued guitar, and muddy feedback-laden guitar were simply adopted into the broader category of **alternative rock**.

Overall, alternative has a much quieter, darker feel to it than the party- and arena-centered hair metal of the 1980s. Alternative often borrows its vocal patterns from grunge, opting for low pitches and mumbled lyrics, and it opts for instrumental accompaniment that highlights the feeling of the song rather than the talents of the artists. Toward the middle of the 1990s, alternative wandered from the darkness of grunge and borrowed influences from many other genres: **Ska** was derivative of the Jamaican genre of the same name, with reggae influences and brass instrumentation; **pop punk** was a simpler, more marketable version of the earlier style after which it was named; **emo** grew out of the same musical roots as punk but featured more emotionally moving lyrics.

A collection of clothing and memorabilia related to Nirvana's "Smells Like Teen Spirit," including Kurt Cobain's sweater, his guitar, and the MTV Video Music Award the video received.

R&B Trends

Much like the changes rock and roll went through, the rhythm and blues of the 1990s would be completely unrecognizable to fans of the genre in the 1950s. Though they shared the same name, the early 1990s style of R&B was much more subdued, tending toward smoother, jazz-influenced vocals with occasional gospel-inspired virtuosic riffs. The trend of new jack swing continued into the new decade, with groups like Boyz II Men and Jodeci offering a more mature, vocally driven version of what the 1980s had to offer. Whitney Houston who had achieved fame in the 1980s with pop hits like "How Will I Know" and "So Emotional" also aged her style with her audience: by the mid-1990s, she had adopted a more serious, adult style of ballads that showed off her impressive vocal power and talent for singing in a melismatic style. **Melismatic** singing extends one syllable over several notes, showcasing the singer's lung power and vocal flexibility. The style was adopted and popularized by many other up-and-coming singers of mid-1990s including Celine Dion and Mariah Carey.

Mariah Carey

Mariah Carey grew up in New York, the daughter of an aeronautical engineer father and a voice teacher mother. Her mother's operatic training helped her navigate and perfect her use of the **whistle register**. The whistle register is the range of notes at the top of the natural human voice range, and it earns its name from the distinct difference in sound (like a whistle) between it and the modal/full vocal range. Carey used her

Mariah Carey's virtuosic vocal style has set her apart for nearly three decades.

well-developed whistle register to set her apart from other singers at the time. She trained the rest of her voice too, perfecting the flashy melismatic style that Whitney Houston was already making popular. Carey eventually met and married Tommy Mottola, the head of Sony Music, and quickly became one of their most popular artists. Carey's self-titled debut album spawned four number-one Billboard hits with her ballad-driven, modern R&B sound. The album's lead single, "Vision of Love," is considered one of the definitive songs of late 1980s/early 1990s pop and R&B. The instrumental components sound dated to a modern listener, heavy on synthesized chimes and keyboards, but the vocal elements are truly timeless. Carey herself recorded the backing vocals, spanning an astounding three octaves over the span of the song. While other singers were competing with each other's melismatic, highly ornamented vocals, Carey's use command of the whistle register pushed the contest even further.

Her next album, *Emotions*, was slightly less successful, but featured a number of more upbeat, danceable hits than its predecessor. Carey's soulful, strong vocals made her a natural at gospel-style ballads, but she yearned to branch out and incorporate a more youthful sound into her future projects. Her professional relationship with Mottola mandated that he have creative control over her image and song choice, and his decisions heavily favored the more serious, mature sound she'd started with. After her divorce from Mottola in 1998, Carey reinvented herself as a sexier, breathier singer who relied upon her music videos to push her new image. Her next album, *Butterfly*, was the first, on which she had full creative control. *Butterfly's* lead single, "Honey," incorporated a hip-hop based instrumental full of samples, drum machine beats, and rapped interludes. Critics appreciated Carey's stylistic flexibility, and though her vocals were still praised, they weren't the main focus the way they had been in her previous work. The song's music video helped Carey communicate her reinvention. For the first time, she featured choreographed dancing and more revealing costumes, establishing herself not only as a vocal icon but as a sex symbol as well.

Hip Hop's Golden Age

Hip hop musical elements like sampling and drum machines made their way into mainstream pop early in the 1990s, helped along by the continued popularity of new jack swing. Hip hop itself was aging gracefully and entering the mainstream as much as rock had in the 1960s. The 1990s was referred to as the **golden age of hip hop** for this reason. Though Tone Lōc released the first rap album to reach number one in the previous year, MC Hammer's album *Please Hammer, Don't Hurt 'Em* smashed previous records in 1990 and held the number one spot for 21 weeks. (It later became the first hip hop album to be certified Diamond by the RIAA, selling a total of 22 million copies as of 2018.) Vanilla Ice's single "Ice Ice Baby" was the first rap song to top the mainstream singles charts the same year. Mainstream pop artists took notice and, like Mariah Carey, many incorporated hip hop musical touches and even rapped verses into their music.

The same year MC Hammer and Vanilla Ice reached mainstream fame, and many more hip hop artists were creating new sounds and styles within the genre. A Tribe Called Quest's debut album, *People's Instinctive Travels and the Paths of Rhythm*, drew upon hip hop's jazz and R&B roots with distinctive samples that hearkened back to those sounds. The lyrics were a departure in hip hop as well, focusing on philosophy, politics, and everyday life rather than the party-driven themes of previous popular hip hop hits. The album's sophisticated lyrics, complex instrumentals, and laid-back feeling inspired many hip hop artists later in the decade as the genre continued to mature.

Lauryn Hill

Among the artists inspired by A Tribe Called Quest's more jazz-oriented, philosophical approach to hip hop was a singer and rapper named **Lauryn Hill**. Hill grew up in New York and was raised in a musical family. She began singing at an early age, appearing on the talent show *Showtime at the Apollo* at the age of thirteen, and even started her school's gospel choir. In high school, she met Prakazrel Michél, who adopted the stage name Pras. The two formed a musical group called "Tranzlator Crew," in which Hill sang and Pras rapped. Pras's cousin Wyclef Jean eventually joined the group as well and the group changed their name to "Fugees" (though they are sometimes referred to as "The Fugees"). Hill eventually learned how to rap so she could be featured just as prominently as her male bandmates. She was particularly moved by the rap styles of male rappers like Ice Cube, who had a more straightforward and blunt delivery than the melodic and playful female rappers of the time. The Fugees released their first studio album in 1994 to little mainstream acknowledgment, but plenty of intrigue from industry insiders.

In 1996, the Fugees released their second studio album, *The Score*. Unlike other hip hop acts of the time, the Fugees wrote a number of hip hop and rap covers of earlier hits, like Bob Marley's "No Woman, No Cry" and Roberta Flack's "Killing Me Softly." "Killing" proved to be the band's biggest hit and was a landmark in hip hop minimalism: the instrumental features only a looped drum beat and a brief sitar riff borrowed from A Tribe Called Quest's "Bonita Applebum." The rest of the song is filled in with echoed vocal harmonies, rap outbursts, and Hill's melismatic, soul-influenced vocals. The song topped the charts worldwide and earned the group a Grammy award in 1997, though conflicting stylistic directions led to the group breaking up later that year.

Determined to make the music she wanted to, Hill began production on what would be her first and only solo album, *The Miseducation of Lauryn Hill*, later that year. The album was the most critically

Despite her runaway success at the 1999 Grammys, Lauryn Hill has yet to release another solo album.

celebrated of 1998, with political and feminist overtones in its lyrics and a vast array of seamlessly blended musical influences. The song "Superstar" references The Doors' "Light My Fire," "Forgive Them Father," and "Lost Ones" feature Jamaican creole influences, and a cover of "Can't Take My Eyes Off of You" (originally performed by Frankie Valli and the Four Seasons) is reimagined with a hip hop beat underneath it.

The album's biggest hit and first single, "Doo Wop (That Thing)" was only the tenth single to debut at number one on Billboard's Hot 100 and was the first debut single to do so in history. The song is a genius modern rearrangement of doo wop and soul musical references. The introduction features a simple piano accompaniment under Hill's vocals (reminiscent of the sparseness of "Killing Me Softly") before giving way to a drum beat and hits of brass to punctuate the ends of the vocal lines. Hill raps the verses and sings the choruses. The music video for the song acknowledges its musical roots. The left side of the screen features Hill performing the song at a block party in the 1960s with a soul band behind her. The right side shows her performing to a contemporary crowd at a block party in the 1990s with modern accompaniment. The reference to block parties is a nod to hip hop's roots in New York, and the split-screen highlights the duality of the song's sound and the permanence of its message. Hill never released another solo album after *Miseducation* (despite fan outcry for nearly 20 years), but her contributions to 1990s hip hop completely changed the direction of the genre and popular music in general.

Country in the 1990s

Country continued to see a rise in popularity entering the 1990s, though its style was changing drastically. Performers like Garth Brooks fused country vocals and lead instrumentals with a rock backing band to give it a bigger sound and a more universal appeal. Reba McEntire, who first came to prominence in the early 1980s, released the pop-country album *Rumor Has It* in 1990. Though country traditionalists didn't like it, its mainstream style along with Brooks's rock-driven country were early indicators of the overall movement of country music that decade. Traditional "honky tonk" style vocals and steel guitar sounds were used rarely if at all. Fiddle sounds remained prominent, but mainly as stylistic accents as opposed to constant accompaniment. Vocals tended more to the pop and gospel style with a country-influenced drawl.

The 1990s was a golden age for women in country music. As previously mentioned, Reba McEntire started to attract mainstream appeal in 1990 and continued to do so, earning ten Grammy nominations over the course of the decade. Trisha Yearwood's "She's in Love with the Boy" was the first debut single by a female artist to hit number one on the country charts, and she continued to enjoy massive success over the next ten years as well. Pop-oriented country took over in the later part of the decade, with artists like Shania Twain and Faith Hill achieving immense crossover success in the pop charts as well.

© lev radin/Shutterstock.com

Shania Twain was the most successful female country artist of the 1990s.

While musical trends from the 1990s largely continued into the first decade of the 2000s, they were met with a drastically different music industry. American homes were first connecting to the Internet at the turn of the century while it was still largely unregulated. Music fans used this new technology to their advantage and the music industry was forced into a dramatic period of readjustment.

File Sharing and Napster

At the end of the 1990s and beginning of the 2000s, most music in the United States was purchased on compact discs, or **CDs**. Listeners began to copy the song files stored on the CD (usually **mp3 files**) to their computer for ease of listening, and for the ability to send the files to others who might be interested. In 1999, a computer programmer named Shawn Fanning developed a program called **Napster** that allowed for file sharing between anyone who installed the software.

© 360b/Shutterstock.com

Napster's popularity forced the music industry to rethink how it made money in the early 2000s.

With Napster, instead of simply sharing the files with their friends and family, anyone in the world could upload and search for files they wanted. Aside from the initial investment of the original uploader in buying the CD, this essentially enabled free music for anyone who belonged to the service. Napster started small among hundreds of students in the Northeastern University, but it eventually peaked at twenty-six million individual users less than two years after its creation.

The prospect of "free" music understandably disturbed the music industry. Throughout the 1990s, physical copies of albums sold incredibly well—helped along by the fact that most music fans bought CD copies of albums they already owned on cassette. Record companies panicked and scrambled for a solution. The Recording Industry Association of America (or the **RIAA**), a trade organization to which most larger record companies belong, began suing file sharing companies that allowed for the illegal distribution of copyrighted music. Many high profile musicians, such as Madonna and Dr. Dre, fully supported these lawsuits and even got involved. (Madonna in particular recorded a track of herself asking, "What the f--- do you think you're doing?" then uploaded it on several popular illegal file sharing sites and programs. She titled it "American Life" after her forthcoming album, hoping to trick file sharers into downloading the insult track instead of the actual album.) In 2000, the RIAA sued Napster for its negative financial effect on record sales and for enabling massive copyright infringement. The RIAA won, and though Napster appealed, the file sharing service shut down in 2001. Napster has since returned as a legal music service, but it has never regained the popularity it had at its peak.

The RIAA's claim of lost revenue is valid: it's estimated that over the span of 1999–2009, physical album sales dropped from $14 billion to about $6 billion. However, the Napster phenomenon did come with its upsides. Releasing unauthorized copies of songs or albums before their official debut (also referred to as **leaking**) could often have a positive effect on sales. For instance, when Radiohead's album *Kid A* was leaked ten months prior to its official debut, the early praise it earned led to it becoming the band's first number one album in the United States. Artists like Kanye West learned to take leaks in stride: when his 2003 debut album *The College Dropout* was leaked prior to release, he used the feedback to edit and perfect it before its official debut.

The fight against leaks and RIAA's lawsuit against Napster didn't completely shut down illegal file sharing, but it did mark the beginning of the recording industry's response to the new digital era. Record companies were forced to accept that physical copies of albums were on the way out, and they would have to move to a digital format to best serve the public's needs.

iTunes, Streaming Services, and New Sources of Revenue

The technology company Apple released the portable digital media player known as the **iPod** in 2001, and alongside it they included the music library and player application known as iTunes. Initially, the devices were unpopular due to their high price and exclusive use with other Apple products. However, with the recording industry's fight against illegal file sharing raging on, Apple saw an opportunity for expansion. In 2003, Apple introduced the **iTunes Store**, an online marketplace through which users could purchase and download individual songs at low prices. This new, legal music downloading service attracted millions of users and drove the iPod to the height of its popularity. Other companies followed Apple's lead, with Microsoft introducing the Zune player, SanDisk releasing the Sansa, and many others capitalizing on the trend.

Still, some music fans desired more freedom and access to a larger catalog of songs than just the ones they chose to purchase. **Streaming music services**, which offer a large library of songs that can be accessed at any time, gained major popularity at the end of the decade. Pandora Radio and Spotify, introduced in 2004 and 2008, respectively, offer their libraries with a monthly subscription, effectively eliminating the need to purchase specific tracks or albums. Apple continues to offer music for sale through the iTunes Store, but now also offers their own in-house streaming service called Apple Music as a response to Pandora and Spotify's popularity.

iPods and other portable digital media players helped facilitate the shift from physical music purchases to digital downloads.

All of the changes brought about by Napster resulted in an entirely different music industry after the first ten years of the new century. Album sales were the most important indicator of an artist's success in the twentieth century, but by 2010 those figures became a small part of a much bigger picture including streaming revenues, licensing, and concert ticket sales.

Popular Music in the 2000s

While artists adapted to the digital trends of the new century, they also updated the musical trends of the 1990s. While the nineties popularized alternative rock, vocally driven R&B, socially conscious hip hop, and female driven country, the 2000s brought their own spin on the previous trends and introduced a few new ones as well.

The Rise of Teen Pop

After two successful decades, MTV had cemented itself as the arbiter of teen taste in music. Artists like Madonna and Michael Jackson were early hits for the channel due to their dance skills, catchy hooks, and provocative lyrics. The end of the 1990s and beginning of the 2000s saw a revival of that trend in the rise of **teen pop**, or pop music specifically marketed to a teenaged audience. In 1999, new artist Britney Spears released the music video for her debut single, " . . . Baby One More Time." In the video, Spears, who was seventeen at the time, performed extensive and provocative dance routines in a Catholic schoolgirl uniform while singing the song's suggestive lyrics. This caused controversy over the sexualization of the underage singer, but like Madonna before

Britney Spears was a central figure in the early 2000s return to teen-focused pop.

her, Spears found that controversy was good for business. Her overnight success opened the door for other teen-focused artists to dominate the pop charts during the early 2000s. A number of teenage female solo singers, including Christina Aguilera and Mandy Moore, launched their careers on the groundwork laid by Spears. Teen pop also saw the return of the **boy band**, a group of male singers singing close pop harmonies. (Despite calling them "bands," most boy band members were singers and did not play any instruments on the group's songs.) The two most popular of these bands were NSYNC and the Backstreet Boys, both formed and managed by Orlando record producer Lou Pearlman. Boy bands employed the same teen pop formula as Britney Spears and her peers: formulaic songs focused on young love and dance-heavy music videos. The teen pop trend died down a bit in the middle of the decade as its fans grew older, but came back in full force a few years later with Disney-backed superstars like the Jonas Brothers and Miley Cyrus. The new crop of teen talent marketed themselves as more serious artists, rarely featuring choreographed dance in their music videos and tending toward playing their own instruments and writing their own songs.

Country

Mainstream country continued to be a girl's world in the 2000s, as it had been in the 1990s. Shania Twain, who had a series of crossover pop-country hits in the 1990s, was the most successful country singer in the early years of the decade. The Dixie Chicks, with quirky lyrics and a more country-rock driven sound, were also incredibly popular. In 2005, the popular television singing competition *American Idol* crowned Carrie Underwood as its first winner to specialize in country music. In addition to country singers finding crossover success, many pop and rock acts had hits on the country charts as well.

Nu Metal, Emo, and Garage Rock

The grunge trend of the early 1990s fully faded into the more marketable alternative rock by the end of the decade. **Nu metal** bands like Korn, Slipknot, and Staind incorporated heavy metal sounds like drop-tuned guitars and dark lyrics into the existing alternative sound. Vocals in nu metal were also drastically different from any previous rock vocal: they often incorporated screaming or growling into the microphone. Some nu metal bands even incorporated hip hop elements into their sound. Rage Against the Machine, Linkin Park, and Limp Bizkit prominently featured rapped vocals over the metal instrumental sound, and the latter two even featured a DJ to scratch and mix samples into their songs. Nu metal's harder lyrics frequently addressed mental health and substance abuse issues, drawing further differences from the original metal styles of the 1980s.

Also popular in the early 2000s was **emo**, short for "emotional hardcore." Emo's sound changed throughout the 1990s and eventually emerged in the 2000s as an offshoot of the alternative movement. Emo borrowed much of its sound from earlier rock genres, but its lyrics were at the heart of the musical movement. As its name implies, emo lyrics are much more emotionally focused and honest. Emo vocal styles can vary from light, folk-influenced sound to punk-influenced screaming, always driven by the content and meaning of the lyrics. Bands like Weezer and Sunny Day Real Estate were early proponents of the heavier punk-influenced sound, but by the height of the genre's popularity bands like Dashboard Confessional had pushed a slightly lighter, acoustic-guitar focused emo sound into the mainstream.

The 2000s also saw a revival in rock's simplest roots known as **garage rock**. The garage rock movement came as a response to the commercialism and hip hop influences incorporated into nu metal. Garage rock bands valued a much simpler sound reminiscent of the 1960s, forgoing much of the electronic mixing and musical elements of modern rock. The White Stripes took this to the extreme. While most bands consisted of at least four members (drums, bass, guitar, and vocals), the White Stripes only had two, with Jack White on guitar and vocals and Meg White on drums. Due to its simplicity, garage rock attracted many rock fans who longed for a less commercial, simpler sound.

R&B Dominates the Pop Charts

Coming out of the new jack swing era of the 1980s and 1990s, R&B saw major mainstream success in the early 2000s. The R&B of the new millennium was more serious, at first featuring far fewer synthesized instrumental elements and showcasing vocal power and harmony. Male singers, who were often overlooked in 1990s R&B, rose in popularity as well. Usher Raymond, known by his stage name Usher, was the most commercially successful solo singer of the decade. Usher's unique soulful voice was powerful and emotional, with virtuosic use of melisma like the R&B divas of the previous decade. Usher exhibited an incredibly diverse style, excelling at soul-inspired ballads and at crossover hits featuring prominent hip hop artists of the day.

Solo female singers like Mary J. Blige and Alicia Keys continued in the model of Mariah Carey's early career, pairing powerful vocals with soul-inspired instrumentals. Girl groups like Destiny's Child appealed to a younger crowd, often incorporating disco-inspired instrumental elements, such as the use of orchestral strings and "four-on-the-floor" rhythms. Destiny's Child member Beyoncé Knowles released her own solo album in 2003 and quickly became one of the decade's most successful solo artists in her own right.

Beyoncé

Though she began as one of four singers featured in the all-female vocal group Destiny's Child, **Beyoncé Knowles** broke out as a major force in music and entertainment in the early 2000s. Born in Houston, Texas, Knowles' father and mother recognized her talent for singing at a young age and encouraged her to perform. She and childhood friend Kelly Rowland joined a local all-girl singing group, Destiny's Child, managed by Knowles's father. His demanding dance and singing practice routines whipped the group into shape and eventually landed them a record deal with Columbia Records. The group's first studio album was a modest success and reached the Billboard Top 200. It wasn't until *The Writing's on the Wall,* their second studio album, was released in 1999 that they would see major mainstream success. The group faced a bit of inner turmoil over the next few years with the dismissal of three members and the introduction of Michelle Williams. As the group's lead singer, Knowles faced the brunt of the backlash from her former bandmates and the media.

Destiny's Child's final lineup of Knowles, Rowland, and Williams was its best-known and most successful. Their third studio album, *Survivor*, debuted at number one in May 2001. It earned the group three Grammys and sold over four million copies. Despite this success, the group announced a hiatus later that year so each member could explore opportunities as solo singers. Knowles tried her hand at acting in a handful of films in

© A. RICARDO/Shutterstock.com

Beyoncé Knowles is one of the most successful recording artists of all time, though she rose to prominence as a member of girl group Destiny's Child in the 2000s.

2002 and began work on her own album. *Dangerously in Love*, her first solo studio album, debuted at number one in June 2003. The album was widely praised by critics and earned Knowles five of her own Grammys that year. Destiny's Child briefly reformed and released their final studio album, *Destiny Fulfilled*, in 2004.

Before the end of the decade, Knowles released two more albums that debuted at number one and starred in four more films, including *Dreamgirls*, based on the 1981 Broadway musical of the same name. *Dreamgirls* itself was loosely based on the story of 1960s girl group The Supremes, whose group dynamics mirrored those of Destiny's Child. In 2008, she married rapper and businessman Jay-Z. Knowles's career has continued to boom since: every successive album she has released (as of 2018) has debuted at number one in the Billboard 200, she has won a total of nineteen Grammys as a solo artist, and her style continues to evolve.

Hip Hop

Hip hop's golden age in the 1990s led to a complete industry takeover in the 2000s. As previously mentioned, rap vocals and DJ-produced instrumentals made their way into nu metal tracks, bridging the gap between two drastically different genres. Rap bridges were popular features in R&B songs in the early 2000s, and were eventually commonplace in mainstream pop songs by the end of the decade. Popular rappers and hip hop producers of the early 1990s were now moguls in the industry, with previous stars running their own record labels and scouting new talent. The once-popular New York and Los Angeles scenes were now less prominent, with Southern and Midwestern rappers coming to the forefront over the course of the decade.

Dr. Dre (born Andre Young) previously belonged to prominent gangster rap group N.W.A., but became the head of Aftermath Records in the early 2000s. Aftermath had a rocky start in the mid-1990s, but hit its stride when Dr. Dre discovered Eminem, the stage name of rapper Marshall Mathers. Hailing from Detroit, Michigan, Eminem grew up in a broken home and used music and wordplay to cope. His natural skill with intricate rhyme schemes caught Dr. Dre's ear and he signed him to Aftermath immediately. Initially, Dr. Dre endured some backlash over hiring a white rapper, though it didn't last long. Eminem's first album with Aftermath, *The Slim Shady LP*, sold over three million copies that year and made him the most prominent star in rap. His stardom was not without controversy, however. The album's graphic, disturbing lyrics led to boycotts and outrage from various groups. Rather than shy away from the shocking content, Eminem embraced it as a trademark and included even more on his next album, *The Marshall Mathers LP*. The rapper's popularity waned in the middle of the decade as he struggled with sobriety issues, but he returned to the top of the charts in 2009 with his sixth studio album, *Relapse*. Later that year, Billboard named him artist of the decade based upon his selling power: all five of his studio albums that decade reached number one, making him one of the only rappers from the early 2000s to still have a prominent following ten years later.

The music industry's digital conversion over the course of the 2000s led to a very different artistic landscape at the end of the decade. Physical album sales were no longer an important barometer for success. Upcoming artists began to realize that they didn't need the help of a major record label in order to find their fan base, and the trend of "going viral" once again forced the industry to re-evaluate their decades-old marketing and sales tactics.

In the second decade of the twenty-first century, the music industry has seen a major shift in the way it sources its stars, produces its music, and reaches its audience. The popularity of illegal file sharing in the beginning of the century led to more focus on the Internet and its negative effect on music sales, but the Internet has since evolved into a platform for finding new talent, developing a fan, and following and making new music accessible to all.

Video-sharing sites like YouTube and social media sites like Twitter, SoundCloud, and BandCamp have made self-promotion incredibly easy. Artists can cultivate a following rather easily by simply sharing videos or sound clips of themselves performing, and can develop several accounts across multiple social media to reach as many potential fans as possible. With enough shares and followers, artists can gain the attention of major record labels and often a recording contract. One of the most famous cases of viral Internet promotion is pop

Sites like YouTube make music immediately accessible for free, and allow up-and-coming artists to reach potential fans with just a click.

singer Justin Bieber. In 2008, talent manager Scooter Braun happened upon a video of Bieber singing a cover of a song by Ne-Yo on YouTube. He saw that Bieber's videos already had a massive amount of views without professional promotion, so the two worked together over the next year creating even more. Bieber was eventually signed by Island Records in 2008 after a record label bidding war that included high-power music stars like Usher and Justin Timberlake. Bieber's success through viral videos caused a shift in artist promotion going into the 2010s—artists were largely expected to take their promotion into their own hands and market themselves before being signed, rather than expect their label to do it all for them.

Hip Hop in the 2010s

Like the 2000s and late 1990s, hip hop has continued to be wildly successful. As of 2017, hip hop has overcome rock to be the most consumed popular music genre. Hip hop has become even more diverse in style than previous decades, sampling a wide variety of genres in its instrumentals and experimenting even further with electronic elements. Vocal delivery in hip hop has become more relaxed in recent years, with more focus on developing interesting rhymes rather than intricate rhythmic patterns. The use of triplet patterns, in which syllables are delivered in an even three beats, is particularly popular. The prominence of the hip hop producer has also widely expanded in recent years, cultivating their own unique styles rather than suiting the artists and even including audio watermarks on tracks they've mixed.

One of the most influential social media platforms in modern hip hop has been SoundCloud. SoundCloud allows artists to upload audio files for online sharing and, more recently, for monetization. While a variety of hip hop artists have shared their music on the site, a particular style has grown incredibly popular there. So-called "SoundCloud rappers" largely share the same aesthetic: simple instrumentals with few layers, obscure samples, electronic effects in the vocal delivery, and lyrics that focus heavily on drug use and criminal activity. A few SoundCloud rappers have achieved mainstream success, including Post Malone and 21 Savage.

Hip hop has benefitted greatly from the use of social media, with many of the decade's biggest stars cultivating their own underground following before being signed or enjoying mainstream success. Some artists, like Chance the Rapper and the collective Odd Future, elected to stay unsigned well after becoming household names. Kendrick Lamar, one of the biggest stars of the decade, spent a large portion of his early career without being formally signed to a record label as well.

Kendrick Lamar

Kendrick Lamar Duckworth, known widely by his stage name Kendrick Lamar, has been one of the most influential artists in the development and advancement of modern hip hop. Born in 1987 in Compton, California, Lamar was raised amid the poverty and police brutality that inspired some of the greatest gangster rap artists of the late 1980s and early 1990s. From an early age, he recognized the importance of music to make cultural and political statements. Though the popularity of gangster rap glamorized gang involvement in the 1990s, Lamar understood it as a last-resort choice among people in his neighborhood to protect their loved ones and make ends meet. Many of Lamar's songs focus on this concept. One of his first songs to achieve widespread popularity was 2010's "Ignorance is Bliss," where Lamar describes different instances of gang activity and then says, "Ignorance is bliss," indicating that many young people involved in gangs do so due to hopelessness to change their situation. It was this song, and the mixtape on which it was released, that caught the attention of Dr. Dre. Much like he had discovered Eminem in the early 2000s, Dr. Dre saw Lamar's complex lyrics and elegantly composed instrumentals as a refreshing change. The two worked together on a number of occasions, but Lamar did not sign with Dr. Dre's Aftermath Records until 2012, nearly two years after they'd first met.

Lamar's first major-label album, *good kid, m.A.A.d city,* debuted in October 2012 and was certified Platinum the next year. The album artfully showcases his range as an artist: the minimally produced "Backseat Freestyle" features Lamar's skill as a lyricist with complicated rhyme schemes and extensive vocabulary; the romantic rap ballad "Poetic Justice" features fellow rapper Drake and uses multiple samples from Janet Jackson's 1993 hit

Kendrick Lamar's brand of politically and socially aware hip hop draws on the roots of gangster rap and Golden Age hip hop and translates them for a new generation.

"Any Time, Any Place"; and the darkly hypnotic "Swimming Pools (Drank)" utilizes a muffled instrumental and alternately slowed and sped-up vocals to musically represent the rapper's struggles with alcohol earlier in his life.

Lamar branched out to different musical influences in his 2015 follow-up album, *To Pimp a Butterfly*. *Butterfly* debuted at number one, despite being released a week earlier than announced. Lamar's style had advanced since his previous album, featuring more experimental rhythms, jazz-influenced instrumentals, and musical references to 1990s golden-age hip hop. His lyrics became more pointed and political as well, broadening his scope to include commentary on institutionalized racism and police brutality. His most recent release as of 2018, *Damn*, was released to wide critical acclaim for balancing the deeply personal sound of *good kid* and the political overtones of *Butterfly*, for a more nuanced, but no less damning look at American society. The album was the first nonclassical or non-jazz work to receive the Pulitzer Prize for Music for its complex lyrics and composition.

Country in the 2010s

Like other popular genres in the past decade, country has embraced a wide variety of outside influences and incorporated many of its past sounds as well. Many country artists have experienced wide crossover appeal, namely Taylor Swift. Swift began the decade as a country artist incorporating pop elements, but largely shifted into mainstream pop as the decade wore on. Others have remained rooted in country sounds but enjoyed widespread popularity, like Lady Antebellum, Blake Shelton, and Carrie Underwood.

An interesting combination of hip hop instrumental influences and country sound emerged at the beginning of the decade and came to be known (somewhat derogatorily) as **bro-country**. Bro-country received its name

Country singer Chris Stapleton's music revives the older blues-influenced style of previous generations.

from its male-focused lyrics and mainly male vocalists. Bro-country artists draw lyrically upon many of the same influences as the party rap of the early 2000s, making frequent reference to drinking, women, and partying. Musically, though the country-style twang-infused vocal and traditional instruments remain, the addition of electronic elements and hip hop rhythmic elements give bro-country a unique twist unlike any previous crossover genre. Music critics and country traditionalists typically dismiss bro-country as repetitive and unimaginative, but the style remains hugely popular among country music listeners.

In direct contrast to the bro-country movement, many artists like Chris Stapleton and Zac Brown Band have embraced the traditional sounds and styles of older country. Stapleton, in particular, fuses modern country with blues-influenced vocal and song styles to hearken back to some of the genre's earliest stars like Patsy Cline and Hank Williams, Sr. Zac Brown Band features some of the more traditional instruments of early country, at times featuring the steel guitar, mandolin, banjo, and even the upright bass. Like hip hop, country has become a much more musically diverse genre since the 1980s and encompasses many more styles today than it ever has.

Pop and R&B in the 2010s

Since 2010, R&B has become one of the main driving forces in popular music. With many of the most popular R&B artists of the 2000s outselling the most successful strictly pop acts, the two genres have been effectively fused. Beyoncé continued her domination of the pop world with her concept albums *Beyoncé* (2013) and *Lemonade* (2016). Rihanna, who enjoyed breakout success in the previous decade primarily as an R&B artist, has since become one of the world's most prominent pop artists. Bruno Mars, who fuses many soul and R&B influences with disco and pop, has also been particularly successful.

Once of the most powerful influences in modern pop is the rise of electronic dance music and its incorporation into American music. Electronic dance music, or **EDM**, had its early roots in disco, with its synthesized beats and layered sounds. As technology improved, EDM developed a much more complicated sound. **Dubstep**, an electronic dance genre with an emphasis on heavy bass lines, enjoyed major mainstream success in the late 2000s and into the 2010s. By the middle of the 2010s, many mainstream pop artists were working with prominent EDM DJs to produce dance-oriented pop tracks. One of the most popular electronic-dance-infused hits of the 2010s was Rihanna's "We Found Love," produced by EDM DJ Calvin Harris. The song models the musical components of an EDM track: Rihanna's vocal is understated and soft, the lyrics are simple and repetitive (particularly in regard to the hook, which features the song's title), and the completely synthesized electronic instrumental features a melodic upward climb or "build up," followed by the introduction of the full instrumental and bass line, known as a "drop." Rihanna and Calvin Harris collaborated on two more EDM-pop tracks over the next five years and each time found great success. The success of her EDM-focused songs informed Rihanna's work from 2011 on and bled over into the work of other artists.

Lady Gaga

Lady Gaga first came to prominence in 2009 with her heavily electronic pop album *The Fame*. Born Stefani Germanotta in New York City, Gaga began her music career performing in a Burlesque show while singing electronically influenced pop renditions of 1970s hits. She experimented with wild stage antics and costumes, which would become her signature later in her career. She was discovered by pop singer Akon while working as a songwriter, and the two worked together to produce songs for *The Fame*. *The Fame* produced two number-one hits, "Just Dance" and "Poker Face," both of which featured electronic instrumentals and electronic vocal effects.

© Matteo Chinellato/Shutterstock.com

Lady Gaga relied on shocking onstage antics earlier in her career but has since softened her approach somewhat. Here she plays a burning piano at a concert in 2010.

Her next album, *The Fame Monster*, made her a worldwide star. Like Madonna before her, Lady Gaga embraced controversy and used her music videos, outfits, and antics to generate buzz about her music and her persona. *The Fame Monster* was technically a reissue of *The Fame*, but it included many new songs and established a much more well-developed sense of Gaga's musical style. In addition to the album's complex use of synthesized instrumental effects and heavy dance-oriented bass, Gaga's strong vocals set her apart from other electronic-pop artists. The album's lead single, "Bad Romance," is perhaps the best example of this. While most singers of dance-oriented pop provide light, uncomplicated vocals to avoid clashing with the electronic instrumental's intensity, Gaga alternates between powerful belting, spoken delivery, and hushed rhythmic chanting to bring out the song's raw emotion. In 2011, she released her next album, *Born This Way*. While still holding on to her initial electronic edge, Gaga incorporated more live instruments into the mix, featuring piano and electric guitar into songs like "You and I" and "Born This Way." 2013's *Artpop* reincorporated many of the early 1980s-inspired synthesized pop instrumentals of her earlier work, but Lady Gaga's overall style has evolved quite a bit since—including a collaboration with classic crooner Tony Bennett and a musically adventurous album titled *Joanne* in 2016.

The Future of Music

Artists today have countless sources of musical inspiration to draw upon as they create the future. The Internet's effect on artist promotion has made it possible for anyone to develop a fan base regardless of where they live, and it has also made music production software accessible to nearly all that seek it out. Previously, in order to mix and master a track of professional quality, an artist had to hire professional help or be a professional themselves. Now, free programs abound online that allow aspiring producers to mix and edit sound and produce a

K-Pop group BTS has enjoyed worldwide fame over the past year and continue to attract American audiences in particular.

high-quality track from their laptop computer. Recording technology has become smaller and more affordable as well, so even those who don't need heavy production and mixing can still record a song with decent quality.

In addition to providing access to production software and potential fans, the Internet allows for quicker sharing of trends, meaning that styles are evolving faster than they ever have. In addition, foreign trends are much more open to American audiences than ever before. **K-Pop**, Western-style pop created for a Korean audience, has gained popularity among American audiences in recent years and will likely see further integration into American popular music.

Additionally, artists today seek out unlikely and unexpected influences: **Foley** sound effects, or everyday, nonmusical sounds, are becoming an increasingly popular inclusion into electronic instrumentals. One more major change that will likely shake up music distribution is the distinction between free music and paid music. SoundCloud rappers and YouTube stars will likely have to work harder to get noticed after 2018, as Billboard has announced that it will no longer factor "free" music (any music available without a paywall) into its charts. If history is any indicator, however, the people will find a way to work around it (and possibly come up with their own ranking system that knocks Billboard from its position of power).

The only thing that seems certain about the future of music is that it will continue to be diverse and exciting. Music fans and artists have never had such creative control or as much access to each other as they do at this moment. No matter your tastes, you're more likely to find an artist that suits them than ever before.

CPSIA information can be obtained
at www.ICGtesting.com
Printed in the USA
LVHW051737270722
724512LV00003B/9